MW01147713

STATE OF PANIC
A Post-Apocalyptic EMP Survival Thriller

JACK HUNT

DIRECT RESPONSE PUBLISHING

Copyright (c) 2016 by Jack Hunt
Published by Direct Response Publishing

State of Panic is a work of fiction. All names, characters, places and incidents either are the product of the author's imagination or used fictitiously. Any resemblance to actual persons, living or dead, events or locales is entirely coincidental.

ISBN-13: 978-1537024752
ISBN-10: 1537024752

Dedication

For my family.

PROLOGUE

They were skinheads. It was a neo-Nazi rally. At a glance, there had to have been at least two hundred of them filling up Main Street in the small town of Mount Pleasant, Idaho. Store signs that once advertised products and services were now covered in sprayed swastikas. Broken glass covered the sidewalk. TVs and mannequins had been dragged out and discarded. My eyes drifted from the unruly to what draped from one side of the street to the other.

A sign emblazed with the words, "White Power."

As I lay prone on a rooftop peering through the Armasight Orion 4X night vision riflescope, silhouettes of

7

the angry were a hazy green. I focused in on the target with my finger hovering near the trigger just waiting for the go-ahead. Noise drifted up attacking my senses. Punk music blared from speakers powered by a generator. Glass beer bottles smashed and scattered all over the street like confetti.

At the center of the chaos on their knees were five police officers.

I shifted my vision towards a cluster of skinheads chasing down a regular citizen who tried to escape. They didn't grab him as much as they slammed his body into a wall, then began laying down a vicious beating with steel toe Doc Martens boots.

"Are you seeing this?" I muttered over the radio.

"Don't do anything stupid, Sam. Wait for my word," Murphy replied.

I turned my eyes away from the horror, disgusted by the sight of senseless brutality.

How had it come to this? I wished there could have been another way but the world had gone to hell and it wasn't coming back anytime soon.

From the top of the roof I peered over the tops of buildings to the towering pine trees that hedged in our once tranquil community. Many of the residential homes were set ablaze. Hot, orange tongues flickered in the night sky. Smoke carried on the wind stung my nostrils. My mind drifted back to the way things were before the event that changed the United States.

Mount Pleasant was nestled beneath I-90 in northern Idaho's Silver Valley. Known for its lumber, mining history and all-season recreation, it had gained the name Pleasant for being exactly that — pleasant. With a population of eight hundred and thirty people, there wasn't much that happened in the town that wasn't known by someone. Word traveled fast. Bad reputations lingered.

Our mountainous region attracted all manner of outdoor enthusiasts from around the globe. With deep powder ski hills, bicycle trails and clear alpine lakes, our town was a haven for the heart seeking solitude. Though now it was far from being anything else but anarchy.

My eyes scanned the tops of the mom-and-pop stores to make sure the others were still there. The shadowy figures of Luke and Edgar were in place waiting for Lieutenant Murphy to tell them when. I thought about Corey, Billy and the others back at City Hall. So much had changed since we had met over a month ago. Though we all came from the same town, we were strangers to one another and for a while even enemies. However, now we were bonded under the same unfortunate circumstances.

Our story started long before the United States screwed up or white supremacists retaliated. And though the odds were stacked against us, there was comfort in knowing that we were in this together. No matter what happened — if we lived or died, our short lives would count for something.

The radio crackled.

"Take the shot," Murphy said over the radio.

His voice sounded like a distant murmur, smothered by the memories of the past.

"Sam. Are you listening? Do it now."

Again the voice of Murphy barely registered as he made several attempts to get through to me. My mind was lost in the arguments, the years of being bounced around foster homes and my abrupt arrival in Mount Pleasant at the age of fifteen. Two years had passed since that day, and not much had changed. In fact life had continued to spiral out of control. The situation I now found myself in seemed almost fitting. My tarnished track record was only made worse by another stint of trouble with the law over possession of drugs with the intent to sell. And with my latest foster family on a crusade to save me, they agreed with the court order that required attending Camp Zero, a local Wilderness Correctional Camp. It was meant to be my last chance at turning my life around before I reached adulthood.

Escorted to the location blindfolded, I was told that disorientation prevented runaways. Operated by three locals, two ex-military guys and a police officer, the camp was located somewhere up in the isolated Selkirk

Mountain Range of northern Idaho. Though the camp had been in operation for no more than two years, it didn't take long for the place to gain a name for itself, because of the results it delivered. Camp Zero was in the business of do-overs. It was initially started as a summer camp for youth whose parents didn't have the patience or time to oversee their antics during summer's months. Over time it evolved and the focus shifted to helping troubled youth.

By troubled, they meant those who had abused alcohol or drugs, were beyond the control of parents, experienced low self-esteem, were rebellious, angry, and defiant or had frequent run-ins with the law. Those who had been suspended or expelled, assaulted others or stolen. The ones who acted out because they suffered from ADHD, chose wrong friends or were socially inept. They accepted the bright but underachieving, the impulsive or hyperactive, the depressed, suicidal, emotionally troubled or simply those who had poor academic achievement.

No one was beyond the reach of being helped.

In their minds, Camp Zero was all about change. At least that was the spiel we got when I arrived a month ago. How long I was meant to be there was unknown. The program was open-ended. Usually it was a couple of months but that was cut short by the blackout.

"Sam! Take the shot!" Murphy's voice bellowed over the radio snapping me back into the present chaos.

The finger trembled. My heart slammed against my chest. I'd never killed anyone before. I never had a reason to. My breathing became rapid as I tried to think of any other way this could be avoided. As I brought my finger closer to the cold metal, I glanced at the small black swastika tattoo on the inside of my wrist. A wave of regret washed over me. What had I done? They had drawn me in with open arms and talk of brotherhood and purpose. Of course, it was all bull, just a mask to hide the hate, racism and disdain for anyone who opposed. I knew that now but it was a little too late.

I brought my right eye back to the scope, and focused in on the chest of the skinhead.

I knew my target. My head shook slightly. It could have been me down there.

A moment's hesitation; uncertain if I could do it.

"Take the shot!" Murphy deafened me with his yell.

One final glance at the officers on their knees.

If I didn't take action now they would die.

I swallowed hard. *Oh God forgive me.*

A slow steady exhale from my lungs.

Then I squeezed the trigger.

CAMP ZERO

1 DAY BEFORE BLACKOUT
CAMP ZERO, NORTHERN IDAHO

Lt. Scot Murphy had taken our group of twelve hiking in the Selkirk Range when the fight erupted. Murphy moved quickly from the front of the line to the back while Officer Kate Shaw and Dan kept an eye on the rest of us.

"Hand it over!" Corey Logan loomed over Billy Manning who was on the floor nursing a cut lip.

Corey Logan. Now there was a guy with some issues. By the age of sixteen he had already assaulted four people and stolen multiple cars. His father had left him when he was six and with his mother holding down two jobs just to make ends meet, anything he couldn't get his hands on he stole. Trying to stop him was a fool's game. For sixteen he was tall. He towered over the rest of us with more meat on his bones than the four of us put together. He said it was muscle of course. No one argued. When he wasn't reminding us of how this place was a prison, he kept to himself. Seeing him in the wilderness squatting down I had a sense that the guy was like a sleeping lion. You might have thought you could get something by him but if he caught you, you were screwed.

"Alright, break it up. What's going on?"

"That pocketknife you guys gave me. He stole it out of my backpack."

Corey had earned the privilege to carry one over the past week by demonstrating that he was capable of not only performing simple tasks like starting a fire, reading a map or completing the asinine assignments we were given, but he had shown a sense of leadership in trying to help others to do the same. Though some might wonder what it was like in that first month. Let me just say, some of those tasks weren't bad. We were taught how to toss a tomahawk at a tree, fire a bow and whether it was a mistake of theirs or not, they even gave each of us a chance to fire off a few rounds at a bunch of cans. Not that we hadn't done that before. Hunting was big in Idaho and if you weren't raising hell in your local town, a person might be found hunting. It was one of the first things my foster parent Brett had introduced me to. I think he thought it was a good way to bond. I just saw it as way to let out pent-up frustration. But there was definitely something about driving out to the mountains, with four-wheelers and camouflaged canoes that felt good.

Anyway, some might have said that handing a pocketknife to anyone at a camp for delinquents was idiotic. And they wouldn't be far wrong. I had to admit it went completely contrary to what other places might have done but there was something about the approach they took with us that made us feel respected. That or perhaps it was because everyone was shit scared of Murphy and Dan. Ex-military guys, built like Spartans with a few rough edges, they carried themselves in a way that made you think twice before pissing them off.

Even with us knowing their history it didn't stop some of the guys from acting like dicks.

"Did you take it, Billy?"

Billy stared back at Murphy for a few seconds then fished around in his pocket. He held up the knife. "You want it?" He tossed it a few feet away. "Go get it." Corey gave him a strong kick in the shin before shuffling away to find it.

"Don't say you didn't deserve that," Murphy said before returning to the front of the line.

What can be said about Billy Manning? He was a scrawny little punk who talked way too much. He was so hyperactive and impulsive, anyone would have thought he was on drugs. Since he had arrived, he had been a constant thorn in the side for everyone. In the first three days he thought he could get himself sent home if he acted like he had mental problems. From taking off his clothes in the middle of the hike and doing a runner, through to pissing on the campfire, the guy knew how to push people's buttons. How the hell he ended up in here and not in a psychiatric facility was beyond me. Billy came from a rich family. His father and mother owned a local logging company. With his father expecting him to work in the business he didn't see the point in schooling so he rarely attended. When he did, he was usually sporting a shiner. No one asked where it came from but most kind of figured it was his father. The guy was as much a lunatic as Billy. A frequent drinker down at Mick's place, a bar on Main Street, he was known for drinking hard, starting fights and heading into the local motel with someone who wasn't his wife. Word got around that Billy caught him in the act and suffered the consequences. The kid couldn't sit down for a week after that. Of course he told everyone that it was a motorcycle accident. We weren't buying it.

Murphy's eyes darted between the two of them. He sighed, took off the skull and bones bandana and used it to wipe the sweat from his forehead. We were six hours into a grueling twenty-mile hike and tensions were riding high. It was to be expected. Frustration led to boredom. Everything had to be earned. Tree bark was used as utensils when eating, backpacks were made from tarp and a pocketknife was only given to those who had demonstrated they could be trusted. Beyond that, we carried only blankets, sleeping bags, a pot and the bare minimum food which none of us liked. In all honesty, it wasn't bad. It consisted mainly of lentils, rice, oats, wheat flour, dried beans, bouillon cubes and dried chili. But after coming off a diet of junk food it was like taking a kick to the gut.

The first week was like hell. From the time I entered we had been told what to do, when to do it and how to do it. Each of us received a list of rules. Do this. Don't do that. That was followed by a complete full-body strip search, which Luke Penn had objected to. When asked to squat and cough, Luke took a shit and then tossed the excrement at Dan.

I had to admit he was a strange dude but he sure broke the ice that day. The others were in fits of laughter. As childish as the act might have seemed, it was his final attempt to kick back at authority.

Luke was in the last year of high school. He was the

kind of guy I saw huddled together with the emos at school. Black hair that hung like curtains over his eyes, black fingernails and more piercings than a person should have. He was a cliché waiting to happen. Suicidal, defiant and angry at everything in life, he kept his distance from the rest of us. One day he was asked to name one thing he liked about life. All he could come up with was jerking off. After which, he flipped Murphy the bird.

When Corey returned from finding his knife, he glared at Billy.

"You know you're not helping yourself, Billy," Shaw said.

Officer Kate Shaw. I knew her well. My frequent run-ins with the law had exposed me to our town's finest. It wasn't a large police department and with the amount of times I had screwed up, it didn't take me long to be introduced to them all. This was her first year helping out with the program. Murphy had made it clear right at the start that she was using her vacation time to assist and if anyone disrespected her they would have to answer to him.

After a thorough strip search, we were each given a set of mundane-looking clothes and boots. Red hoodies, khaki military pants and sandy-colored boots. They wanted us to look the same and act the same to avoid any conflicts.

"Okay, guys, listen up. We are going to camp here for the night. So go ahead and set up your tents."

By tents they meant shitty tarps draped over low-hanging branches. If you didn't tie them down, it would flap in the wind and you'd experience nature up close and personal.

I slumped down onto my knees and rolled back releasing the fifteen-pound weight off my back. All of us groaned and began checking our feet for blisters. The back of my heels were red raw. The first week in the wilderness was brutal. Some of the guys hadn't even set up a tent in their backyard, let alone spent a night with Mother Nature.

"How much longer are you going put us through

this?" Luke asked. "I would kill for a cigarette."

Lt. Scot Murphy — or Murphy as he liked to be called — threw his bag down and went over to Luke and began rooting through his bags.

"What the hell are you doing?"

"Where have you been keeping them?"

"What?"

"The cigarettes."

"I don't have any."

We all looked on with morbid curiosity. It wasn't like when we first got here. Back then every few hours someone in our group took over the reins of playing the clown. Now the honeymoon period had worn off and we just wanted to go home. But that wasn't going to happen under Murphy's watch.

Murphy was an ex-Navy SEAL. A patriot you might say. He knew how to whip someone into shape and had a built-in bullshit detector that worked like magic. Regardless of why each of us was here, I think we all respected him to some degree. The guy knew his stuff.

He'd already shown us that when we thought we had reached our breaking point, we could go further. That's why most days we hiked for miles upon miles. He said it allowed us to think about where we had come from and the choices that had led us to being here. Initially we all just thought he was full of shit and was trying to punish us.

Within a matter of minutes, all of Luke's stuff was scattered on the ground. Murphy began fishing through the sealed-up bags of dry food.

"He has it up his ass," Billy said.

Luke frowned. "Screw you, Manning."

"No, I'm telling you that's where these guys like to store it. I knew a dealer a few towns over that kept his gear inside a tied baggie and then shoved it up his rectum, leaving just a small amount of the bag hanging out. That way if the cops ever raided his place he wouldn't get caught."

"And you know this because?" someone in the group asked.

"Everyone knows it. Isn't that right, Sam?"

"Whatever, man," I replied.

"Alright, get up and head over to the bushes," Murphy said.

"You can't be serious?" Luke protested.

Murphy didn't even need to reply. We had all become accustomed to Murphy's stare. Come to think of it, we had become accustomed to a lot of things that he, Dan and Officer Shaw didn't like. Unlike the people who ran some other correctional camps, these guys didn't get angry or upset at us. They wore us down by not giving in.

We watched Luke trudge off into a thick set of bushes. Billy laid back on his sleeping bag and chuckled to himself. "What a guy."

A few minutes later Murphy reappeared from behind the bush. Using twigs like BBQ tongs, he held out in front of him a small plastic bag full of tobacco and papers. Murphy tossed it on the ground and proceeded to make a fire to burn Luke's private stash. When Luke emerged, he was red in the face and downcast.

"I told you," Billy crossed his arms behind his head and breathed deeply. Truth be told, both of us had used the same dealer. I'd passed by Billy on numerous occasions. Back then we never said a word to each other. That's how I knew there was truth to what he had said. The dealer was pretty straight up about it. Almost boasting that he hadn't been caught because it was an old method used by criminals and no cop in a small town was going to go through the trouble of doing a cavity search. The county didn't pay them enough, he would say.

We all spent the next twenty minutes constructing our makeshift tents out of branches and tarp. They weren't ideal and there had been a few nights it had dropped below zero but they kept the rain off our heads. The only thing I worried about were rattlesnakes. I hated them. The thought of waking up in the night with one of them inside my sleeping bag was disconcerting.

We had set up camp close to the Kootenay River. All of us were involved in gathering wood, cooking and whatever else they wanted us to do.

"So Murphy, you ever had any runners?" Corey asked.

He gazed into fire and prodded glowing embers with the end of his stick. "A couple."

"Did they get far?"

"Nope."

"Why not?"

"Look around you, guys. You want to hike out of here, be my guest. You won't get far."

He was right. After all the walking we had done, by the time we dropped our gear none of us had the strength to try and escape. And there would have been no point. The local cops would have picked us up and brought us right back. Every single one of us was here because the court had ordered it. Murphy and Officer Shaw knew Judge Wickins. They had made some agreement with him to send troubled teens to their camp. So, it wasn't just a case of our parents saying that we were out of control and two months in the wilderness would solve all our problems. We had ruffled the wrong feathers, and even the judge wanted to wash his hands of us.

I stared around at the others. Some of them I had got to know, most kept to themselves and just seemed as if they wanted to get through the program. Corey, Billy and Luke were the only ones that came from the same area as me. The other eight were from surrounding towns.

Before my arrival, I'd heard about the place. Camp Zero had earned a name for itself as the location parents sent their kids if they wanted to see real change. I'd seen Murphy around town picking up supplies or having breakfast with Dan. I just never imagined I would end up here.

"So what's the deal with the women? Why aren't there any babes in this place? No offense, Kate," Billy said.

"None taken."

Kate was rolling out a sleeping bag. I eyed her from across the fire. To us, she was Officer Shaw. However, Billy liked to call her by her first name. The few times I had seen her outside of the station were when she was patrolling our sleepy little town. She was a single mother who had lived her entire life in Mount Pleasant. Her daughter Kiera was one of those sporty cheerleader types who tended to spend more time cheering the jocks on and wiggling her tush more than anything else. I often wondered if it was just a front. With her mother as a cop and all, I imagined she had to keep up appearances, say all the right things and look as if she was excelling. The community of Mount Pleasant was big on keeping up appearances. Town hall meetings every Wednesday usually got quite a turnout, signs up and down the streets were cleaned on a weekly basis, and people mowed their yards to keep up with the joneses. It was sad to think that at one time all those adults had been like us in one way or another.

"There are usually girls here but this last intake we had more guys. We rolled the girls over into the next program."

"Just my luck," Billy said before taking his pot down to the water to rinse out.

"Try not to fall in this time, Billy," Dan said.

"Fuck you," Billy replied.

"That's one more stone."

Billy picked one up. That was another rule. If you swore out here you had to pick up a stone and put it in your bag. Of course this would make it heavier and in turn cause untold frustration, which usually led to more cursing. So far it had turned into a bit of a competition as to who had collected the most stones. Billy currently had taken the lead.

Dan Adams wore a coonskin hat and a checkered shirt. He had one of these odd-looking mustaches that drooped down the sides of his mouth and off the edge of his chin. He looked every bit at home in the wilderness as would a squirrel. A longtime friend of Murphy's, Dan had been a medic in the military; he usually would recount stories of his time in the war. Some of the crazy things he had seen. Guys with arms and legs blown off weren't the worst, according to him. It was seeing toddlers sent out towards a convoy of troops with C4 attached to them. When he wasn't making us want to chuck up what we had for dinner, he was cracking jokes.

"So listen, guys. You've been out here a month now. I know for most of you it has been probably the hardest thing you have ever done but I want to tell you that we are proud of you."

"Oh great. Does that mean we can go home now?" Corey asked in a joking manner.

"Sorry, Corey. Not for a long while. We have you for another month and believe me a lot is going to happen in that time. We like to ease you guys into this. That's what the first month is about. Getting you adjusted to taking responsibility. For some of you this is the first time in your life you haven't been filled up with drugs or tobacco and I want to hear from you what that feels like."

"Shit. Yeah, that's about it," someone muttered.

"Well, I doubt Luke here is going to have much to say," Billy remarked before laughing.

"Screw you, Billy."

"Luke, give your mouth a rest," Dan said.

"Who wants to go first?" Shaw asked.

No hands went up. There was near silence. All that

could be heard was the lapping of water against the shore. In the darkness of the forest, wood crackled and popped as ash floated up into the air.

"I'll go," a guy by the name of Zach replied.

"Right on," Dan replied.

"Well." I cleared my throat. "For a program that I thought would have been like military boot camp it's far different than I expected. I'm not saying it's easy but it's definitely allowed me to reflect on some of my decisions."

"Are you sure you're not high?" someone asked. "As this place sucks."

Billy and a few of the others chuckled.

"Quiet down. Who else wants to go?"

Everyone's eyes looked at each other.

"Sure. I'll go," I said.

"Okay good. Sam, what has meant the most to you about this time?"

Luke smirked and tapped a stick against a rock waiting for me to speak.

"I don't know. Maybe a sense of being part of

something bigger than myself."

"In what way?"

I breathed in deeply and gazed into the orange flames. The smell of burnt wood carried on the air brought with it the scent of the forest.

"I've been bounced around foster homes my entire life. You always think the next one is going to be the one."

"And is it?" Murphy asked. "I mean, the one you are in now?"

"I think I stopped asking that question a long time ago."

"Do you think your foster parents don't care about you?" Shaw asked.

"Well, I mean they sent me here, didn't they?"

"Right. But doesn't that mean something to you?"

"It means something to me. My father's an asshole," Billy said.

"Billy, if you are not being asked to speak, kindly refrain from opening your pie hole," Murphy said.

"Go on, Sam," Dan urged.

I sucked air in between my teeth. "I don't know." I tossed a twig into the fire and watched it burn up.

"What about that swastika tattoo on your wrist? What does that mean to you?"

I glanced up at Murphy but didn't answer. He knew what it meant but he wanted to hear it from me. The others looked on with curiosity. It wasn't that I was a neo-Nazi sympathizer or anything that someone might have assumed. It was that I had found a sense of belonging among a group that had welcomed me in. Hell, it could have been anyone. It just happened to be them.

"Yeah, are you racist?" One of the black kids in the group spoke up.

"No."

"Then why are you wearing that dumb tattoo?"

"Fuck you, man."

"Oh yeah? You want to go?"

The guy jumped up and before either one of us could throw a punch, Murphy and Dan got in the middle.

"Settle down. I think we are getting away from the

main point here."

"I'm not racist."

"No?" Luke asked. "Then why the tattoo?"

I shook my head and pushed a sleeve down to cover it. "I'm done talking."

"We're just trying to find out where all that hate stems from," Luke added before smiling.

"Well, why don't you come over and I'll show you."

Luke scoffed. "I wouldn't waste my breath on you, skinhead."

"Enough!" Dan pointed at Luke.

"It's okay, Sam," Murphy said. "Who else would like to share?"

I heard the murmurs among the others. Ever since I had shown up at the program with a skinhead and the tattoo there was clear animosity. I ran a hand over my head. It had changed a lot over a month. It wasn't as short, but in their eyes I was still a skinhead. I couldn't blame them really, for before this, that's what I had portrayed myself as. A green bomber jacket, tight jeans, tattoos, hair buzzed off and a mouth and attitude to go with it.

I ran with the skinheads, just as each of the others chose their group. I was no different than them. I carried the same hate as they did for authority. But I was no racist.

In all honesty I didn't know why I got that tattoo, other than I wanted to fit in. And, for a time I had. I scoffed now as I thought back to the day I was busted. The very people I had called my brothers were the ones that left me in the dust.

As the fire burned low and each of us shared something about our time at Camp Zero, I reflected on what Murphy had said about my foster family. Had they sent me here because they cared? Or was it a last resort before they sent me back to child services to be placed with another family? I wasn't sure.

I watched the flames flicker.

"Brotherhood."

"What?" Murphy said as he lay on his sleeping bag

across from me.

"You asked me what it meant. Brotherhood."

"Are you sure about that?" Murphy replied.

BLACKOUT

Dawn began like any other and yet it wasn't any other morning. Unbeknownst to us, today would be remembered in history as the greatest terror attack that the United States had experienced. It would overshadow 9/11 and throw the United States back to a way of living reminiscent of the 1800s.

We awoke at a little after six, just in time to see a deep orange sun rising over the tops of the mountains. A heavy mist lingered in the air making its rays look even more hypnotic. I breathed in the smell of pine and stared at the bubbling river. There was something very serene to being in the wilderness. Whether we knew it or not, it worked away at the noise in our heads. All the voices that told us we needed to be this or that, or had to be doing something more. It asked for nothing except respect. It was peaceful but that peace would be short-lived.

After having breakfast, we packed up and headed back

towards Naples, Idaho, which was where the main office for the camp was. The goal was to collect mail that had been sent to us by our parents and then head back out into the wilderness.

That morning I had tried to pen a letter to my foster parents, Jodi and Brett. They were the eighth set of foster parents that I had since I was four. I never knew my birth father or mother. I only remember being handed off from one family to the next. Each time it was the same. I ran away, caused problems at home or was expelled from school. None of them were ready to deal with my antics and I wasn't really sure how to behave. One doctor said it was a chemical disorder, another a mental illness. Others said it wasn't any of those things. They notched it up to drugs and running with the wrong crowd.

I don't know what it was. I gave up a long time ago figuring it out. It was easier to agree with child services and hope that the next home was better than the last. The fact was, most of the families were just taking kids in to make some extra money. I was meant to be seen and not heard. Eventually I just decided not to be seen.

Jodi and Brett were different in more ways than one. They were African Americans. They didn't have a son or daughter like previous families. They had tried to have kids and for whatever reason couldn't. Fostering wasn't something they did for the check. At least that's the impression I got. They honestly seemed to care. Maybe that's what freaked me out. I had become so used to being beaten with a belt, sexually abused or cursed at, that any degree of care caused me to question motive. I still wasn't sure what theirs was.

Murphy was the only one who didn't try to label me. Instead, he listened and posed questions. He was the first, along with Dan and Shaw that attempted to help me see them as family.

Once a week we picked up letters. There was always one there from Brett. I never read it. I stashed the letters inside my bag. Instead I would watch the others react to the letters they received from the same people who put them here. Well, it wasn't the parents, it was the court but the parents approved of it. So in my books, it was Brett and Jodi who sent me here. At first I took offense to that decision. But slowly I was beginning to see that maybe it was for the best.

Those I ran with weren't die-hard supremacists. At least I didn't think so. More like wannabes hoping to impress an older generation who were more committed. I had met the group through a local martial arts dojo. The head honcho, or guy that was in charge, was using the place as a means to recruit younger kids. I was fifteen when I was introduced to them. Two years later I earned my red laces. It's hard to say at what point I stepped over the line. The indoctrination was subtle. We'd meet every week in the basement of the dojo, listen to punk music, get drunk and they would talk about having a pure race.

To be honest, most of what was said went in one ear and out the other. I didn't agree with them. I couldn't wrap my head around why being a Jew, black, or whatever, mattered. It was immaterial to me. No, I was there because they welcomed me in. That was it. Hell, I was pretty sure if a local religious group in town had befriended me I would have walked down a very different path to the one I was on. But that never happened. I fell in with the wrong crowd, the judge said. And for that I was here to a pay a price.

We hiked from seven in the morning until one in the afternoon. By the time we arrived at Camp Zero's headquarters, the sun was beating down on us. All of us were exhausted and ready to call it a day. But we knew it was just the beginning of another long hike out into the harsh wilderness.

Murphy unlocked the door and instinctively hit the light switch. A generator kicked in and fluorescent lights flickered before turning on.

"That's odd."

"What?"

"The generator kicked in."

"Maybe it's blown a fuse," Shaw replied.

Dan had gone off to collect the mail from the box while Officer Shaw tried to keep us quiet. Everyone was grumbling about having to hike any further.

"You think we could spend the night here? You know we've been hiking non-stop over the past month, up and down the mountain range, through the forests. I'm all for taking in a bit of nature but this is like overkill. Are you trying to kill us?"

"I second that, my feet are killing me."

We hadn't showered or shaved in several weeks and all of us stunk to high heaven. The only way we could clean ourselves was when we were close to a river. And no one was brave enough to endure the icy cold water on their nutsack.

"My back feels like it's about to break."

Murphy came back out with a big case of water. "Dear god, you guys wouldn't last a day in the military."

"That's why I'm not joining," Billy said.

"I don't know, I kind of like the idea of seeing the world," Corey added.

"Dude, you aren't going to be seeing the world. Just bullets flying over your head, and knowing your fat ass they wouldn't have any problems painting a target on you."

Corey stuck his finger out. "I swear I'm going to…"

"Going to what?" Billy tossed off his backpack and leveled up to Corey which was kind of insane really. They were like David and Goliath. I had to hand it to Billy though, the kid had some balls, especially after having been slapped down by Corey three times over the past month already.

"Settle down."

They both glared at each other and turned away.

Dan returned with the mail and began sorting through it. He tossed some of it out to different guys and then tucked the rest into his back pocket.

"Anything for me?" Luke asked.

"Not this time."

"Kind of figured," he replied. "Hey Murphy, you got any cigarettes in there?"

"What did I tell you?"

He shook his head in frustration. Nicotine addiction

44

was a bitch. I felt his pain. I had gone through the whole aching for a cigarette from the first day we had arrived. They had allowed us to have one before we set out hiking but it was kind of pointless as it only made me need another.

I cracked open a bottle of water and chugged it down then poured the remainder over my head. My body trembled as it ran down my back. The temperature that day was hovering in the high seventies. As they sat around reading letters, I noticed Murphy looked concerned.

"Everything okay, bud?" Dan asked.

"Generator's on."

"And the phone?"

"Phone's not working. Not even getting a signal. Radio is getting static."

I was laid out on the ground trying to get some shuteye while at the same time listening in on the conversation. Murphy went around the side and I saw him fiddling with a gray metal fuse box. He muttered something to Dan and he took a look.

"Listen, I'll take the truck down to the general store and see what I can find out. Might just be a downed line."

"Bring back some beef jerky," Billy hollered. His words fell on deaf ears. Much of what we suggested carried little weight around here.

Letters from parents were usually the same. At the beginning of the program we were encouraged to write to them, tell them how things were going and apologize for our behavior. We weren't forced to do it but some of the group thought if they acted as though they were remorseful, their parents would pull them out. Others pleaded. Some wrote that they had learned their lesson. Of course they were all lying. In the first week I had even done it myself, though I kind of figured it would do little to help me. In the minds of Jodi and Brett Anderson I was a lost cause in need of saving and Lt. Scot Murphy and his crew were the ones to do it.

As a few finished reading, I glanced over to Shaw and Murphy. Both of them were standing a few feet away talking. Despite the fact that nothing appeared to be working, neither of them looked too worried.

I turned my attention to the others who were scattered around the camp. Some sat on the picnic tables chatting while others tried to sneak in a few minutes of sleep. All of us had got used to roughing it over the month. The first few weeks were brutal but once we knew that we were here to stay, it didn't take long for our minds to readjust. Of course we still craved creature comforts but without them in sight, and without technology around us, there was nothing to distract us except the wilderness. Living in the wild was like detoxing from a polluted world. It wasn't just coming to terms with how our actions had landed us here, it was coming to grips with the fact that our entire lives ran off the grid. We were a generation that spent so much time in front of cellphones and tablets and god knows what else, that we were missing out on the very thing that was in our backyard — real life.

An hour later, when Dan returned he was driving

pretty damn fast. The truck careened into the parking area, kicking up gravel. He signaled to Murphy to follow him inside. Shaw remained outside to keep an eye on us. A couple of the guys started causing a fuss and Shaw went over to break it up. Naturally I was curious. I got up and wandered over to the door. It was slightly ajar.

"Are you sure?"

"That's what Jake said. We are under attack. The cities have been hit."

I furrowed my brow and then pushed the door open. "Under attack?"

Dan pointed to me. "Outside. Now."

"No, what's this about being under attack? What the hell are you on about?"

Luke must have overheard me as he got up and wandered over. Now two of us were standing in the doorway badgering them with questions. We weren't stupid. There was no power and I'd heard him correctly.

"Look, just settle down. I don't want anyone freaking out."

"Freaking out? Then tell us what's going on."

Murphy looked at Dan. "You think you can get the ones from—"

He hadn't even managed to get the rest of his words out when outside the others erupted in a collective gasp and cursing. I turned and noticed them looking up and pointing. As I stepped outside, my eyes bulged. Coming down a short distance from us was a 747 plane. Out of control and in a death spin, there was no way that plane was going to pull up.

It was about to crash.

Murphy screamed. "Move!"

The explosion that followed echoed throughout the valley.

HOMETOWN

"Take the Scout II and get them back home. I'll take the others."

"But your vehicle has a computer chip." Dan replied.

"Not the K5 Blazer."

What occurred next was organized chaos. Dan started shouting names and pointing to his van while Murphy went and retrieved a secondary truck from a garage. I dived into the back of Murphy's truck along with Luke, Billy, Corey, three others and Shaw. The rest went in Dan's. They were all from out of town. There were no goodbyes or pats on the back. Just blank stares and a sense of urgency.

A sense of dread crept over us. It was only made worse by the fact that none of us seemed to know what was happening. In the distance black smoke rose in the air from the crash. The only thing mentioned by Murphy was EMP, the rest of the time he was talking to Shaw. We tore out of there leaving a plume of dust in our wake. As the truck rumbled along the road each of us stared behind, occasionally looking up into the sky wondering if it was going to rain planes.

"I've heard of this before. My old man used to talk about terrorists attacking. This is probably one of those biochemical attacks."

"Shut the hell up. It's the power that's gone out," Corey replied.

"That's how it all begins. Power goes down and then a deadly toxin gets released into the air. No one can get out. Hell, look at all the cars we've passed in the last three minutes." Murphy ended up having to go off road due to vehicles clogging up the highway. People were standing outside of the vehicles looking lost and aimless. Others were holding their phones out as if trying to get reception. The few vehicles that didn't have computer chips kept moving.

"The power is down," Billy shouted to a guy on the hard shoulder as we left the road.

Mount Pleasant was south, a good two hours from Naples. We had been traveling on I-90 before Murphy came off the road. While he tried to stay close so that he didn't get lost, I was pretty damn sure he could find a needle in a haystack. The guy knew his way around just by the sun and stars. As we bumped up and down and clung to the sides, I had a feeling that any minute now one of us would be thrown out the back.

"You want to slow down?"

Murphy wasn't listening. I slid forward. "You got kids, Murphy?"

"A daughter."

I frowned looking at his hand. There was no ring on his finger. "You divorced?"

"Yeah."

"What's your kid's name?"

"Ally."

"Ally Murphy?"

He nodded not taking his eyes off the road ahead.

I couldn't believe it. I knew of Ally. I'd seen her

around school. I had no idea that was his kid. Then again I didn't pay much attention to anyone when I did attend.

"What street does she live on?"

"Fairview Avenue."

"West side. Nice area."

"And you?"

"Just take a seat."

I was about to say something when the truck bounced and I hit my head. I groaned. Billy found it amusing but then anything was amusing to that schmuck.

"So who do you think's behind it?" Corey asked Shaw.

"No idea." She was looking down at her phone and checking reception.

"It's got to be ISIS or one of those Middle Eastern countries. All the shit that's going on right now is down to them."

"Maybe not. Hell, it could be our people," Luke said.

"America attacks America? Get out of here, Penn."

"Why not? We have our fair share of radicals. Hell, I've always thought that if this world went to hell, our government would be behind it."

Corey snorted. "Yeah, I'm with you on that."

The truth was it was hard to tell what was going on but whatever had occurred was serious. Certainly the look of concern on Dan's face when he returned was real.

"Listen, all we know right now is that some idiot has probably turned off a switch and screwed up the power grid. Remember when that big outage happened on the East Coast? No one was shouting about a terror attack then."

"Um. We didn't have planes dropping out of the sky."

"One plane. The guy probably dropped his coffee."

"You think that's funny?" Corey yelled at him.

"A little too early?" Billy replied

Corey grabbed hold of him and I dived across to try and intervene. That's when I felt the fist hit me in the side of the face. I had moved too soon and took the full brunt of Corey's right hook. It was like being hit full force with a sledgehammer. Darkness crept in at the corners of my eyes. I blinked hard.

"Holy crap," Billy started laughing. "Thanks, Frost."

Shaw intervened before it spiraled out of control any further. Huddled in the back of the truck, wind whipped at our faces. We passed through several towns on the way. Pandemonium had already set in as people began looting stores. I'd always imagined how America would react to a real disaster but seeing it was another thing entirely. One town we passed through seemed empty. Storefronts were already closed and metal shutters covered the fronts. The next wasn't as lucky. We saw two guys outside brawling over what appeared to be a case of water. The next town a few of the stores had flames coming out of caved-in windows.

"What the hell?" I muttered. Feeling chilled by the air I pulled myself up and slid forward. "Murphy, what did Dan mean by we are under attack?"

He glanced at me in his rearview mirror and exhaled hard.

"Multiple cities in different states all over the country have been hit."

"By what?"

He glanced again at me.

"We're not sure yet but the grid is down."

"How did he find that out if there's no power?"

"I don't know. Maybe word got out before the power went completely down."

I slumped back in my seat and swallowed hard. I looked over to Shaw who was riding shotgun. She stared out without saying a word. How many people had died? What cities had been hit? Questions spun through my mind.

As we saw signs for our hometown I began to feel a little more at ease. I don't know why, as it was about to be completely shrouded in darkness in a matter of an hour. As the truck veered off the main highway and made its way down Front Street, our eyes scanned the stores for trouble. I expected to see people looting but it was reasonably calm.

"Okay, listen up, we will drop you off at your homes. If in the event that you have any problem, I'm going to be down at City Hall seeing if there is anything I can do to help. You got that?"

Murphy dropped off the three kids one by one. We watched them run up to their darkened houses. By now the sun was beginning to wane. When I jumped out at the end of Silver Street, I glanced back at Murphy. We had spent the last four weeks together and whether I wanted to admit it or not, all of us guys had begun to feel a sense of safety around him.

"Remember, Sam. City Hall. Seven o'clock."

I nodded and strolled up the driveway to the house. Inside it was dark even though the sun hadn't completely set. I turned back momentarily as Murphy pulled away. Billy stuck his finger up at me. The guy still saw all of this as one big joke. He only lived ten doors down. Luke was one street over on Maple Drive and Corey a few blocks down from that.

"Jodi? Brett?"

I didn't refer to them as dad or mom, it was too strange. When I was younger I tried the whole mom and dad thing but after family number four I gave up.

In the silence of the home, there was no reply. I slung my bag down and went into the bathroom and turned on the taps. Water was still working. It was freezing cold but at least it was still flowing. I filled up the sink in front of me and stripped down. My body felt grimy and I badly needed a shave. After I had tossed some water and soap under my pits and cleared the forest around my chin, I looked at my scalp. I had a month's worth of growth. It was still short and dark. I tossed the razor into the sink and decided to leave it.

I ambled into my bedroom and slipped into a pair of black jeans and a white T-shirt. I pulled on a hoodie and my green bomber jacket and began to feel more like myself. I dug around inside a drawer for cigarettes but there were none. I tried the next. They had been cleared out. I took a seat on the edge of my bed and I blew out my cheeks as I tugged my boots on.

"Brett?" I called out again. There was no answer.

Wandering into the kitchen, I spotted a note on the

table. Scribbled in blue ink was a message from Jodi.

Sam,

We are at the Robertsons' home on Pearl Street. If you've returned please come over there. The address is 483.

Love Jodi

I paced the kitchen, got myself a drink and fished around in the fridge. It was stocked with food, food that would eventually go off if the power didn't come on soon. I grabbed up my bag and threw in some fruit and a couple of cans of food and then searched around in the drawers for some flashlights and batteries. I glanced at the clock, it was a little after five.

I was heading out the door when I was spotted by one of my old skinhead pals. Bryan Catz.

"Well, shit on me, Frost. Don't tell me they released you early?"

Bryan Catz wore a green bomber jacket, tight jeans and black boots that went up his knees. His bald head sported a spider web that covered the back portion. He had a cigarette sticking out of his mouth and he was with three others.

"What the fuck happened to your head?"

He ran a hand over it and the others started laughing. "You need to shave that shit off."

"I just got back."

"Where you heading now?"

"Check in with my old man."

"Screw that. C'mon. The rally begins tonight."

I pulled back from him. "Rally?"

"Haven't you heard?"

"What?"

"Look around you. This is it, man."

"What do you mean?"

He studied me as if I was from another planet. He slipped his arm around my shoulders and took a hard pull on his cigarette.

"You remember us talking about that missile that hit Germany?"

The United States had set up an anti-missile system in Eastern Europe. Russia and China had kicked up a fuss about its proximity to their countries. The U.S. reassured them that it was to stop Iranian missiles. Russia didn't see it that way and said that it was no different than if they set up one in Cuba. It had turned into a heated political exchange that some were saying would no doubt lead to the next world war.

That only seemed even more real when at some point that system had malfunctioned and several missiles had been fired and hit Germany. Several thousand people were killed causing uproar worldwide. Even though the USA tried backpedaling, it was useless, they had just hit a hornets' nest that had been quietly buzzing. It had occurred a few weeks before I was sent to Camp Zero. The airwaves were filled with talk of retaliation. That if it didn't come from Germany, there was a good chance that Russia would strike.

"Our brothers hit back."

I frowned trying to make sense of what he was saying.

"You? What do you mean?"

"Well, not us directly. Our kind. White power." He leaned in all excited. "Seems they had their hands on nuke bombs from the Cold War. Fucking amazing."

"You're not making any sense."

"There were 84 suitcase nuke bombs that went missing in the Cold War. Let's just say they weren't really missing. They exchanged hands. Each suitcase had a one-kiloton nuclear warhead inside. We are talking about wiping a city off the map, obliterating the power grid and taking out military and satellite defenses."

"Why the hell would they do that?"

"We are taking this country back. This is what it has always been about. We are going to purge this land, every city and every town until all that remains is white power." He began walking with me, gripping my shoulder and talking as though I was still one of them. But everything about what he was saying only disgusted me. Killing innocents? This wasn't just about striking back at blacks or Jews as most assumed white power was about. It was about defeating anyone that stood in their path. It didn't matter if you were white, or any other color of the rainbow. It was about control for power.

"All this time they have been looking at the Middle East and we have been right under their nose slowly gaining ground, just waiting for the right time to strike. This is it. This is our time, brother."

I wanted to tell him that he wasn't my brother but I'd seen what they had done to those who opposed them. I had seen how they had stomped to death those who turned coat. One guy even earned his red laces by stomping to death another who had chosen to hand his in. Turning your back was deemed an act of cowardice; a lack of commitment to the cause and it wasn't tolerated. Sure, there were some that would do nothing to you but not the ones in this town. They were nutcases.

"There's supposed to be over two hundred and forty of us here for the rally."

"To celebrate?" I said trying to act as though I was on the same page as him.

"No, you idiot. We are taking this town." He then tapped me on the shoulder and with his arm still around me pulled my chin up in the direction of the town. I glanced away from him into the distance. Flames flickered up into the early night sky.

"See. We've already begun."

ANARCHY

I had to think fast. They would expect me to go along with them and join in whatever crazy plan they had in store for the evening.

"You hear that? No cops. Come on, we'll be late," he said pulling on me.

In the distance, no siren could be heard. All the cop cars would have had computer chips, fire trucks as well.

"I'll meet you there. I have to check in with my father."

He scowled. "Your father? You've never referred to him as your father."

"I meant Brett."

He studied my face for a moment and I felt a trickle of sweat go down my back. He grabbed hold of my head. "Don't be fucking late." Then he blew smoke in my face and started laughing. I chuckled a little trying to pretend as though I thought he was funny. They walked away occasionally looking back. One of them kicked over a trash can and bags of trash scattered. Another grabbed one and slammed it against a parked car.

They pumped the air with fists and shouted at people passing by. Neighbors ran inside and closed their doors. I watched as they ran up and kicked in a few doors and scared some of the neighbors. They would have never done this before but there were no police around to stop them. Where were the police? My eyes drifted back to the orange and yellow tongues of fire licking at the darkening sky.

I put my other arm through the strap of my bag and took a shortcut through an alley that led down between two houses. It took me over a small creek and up a grass-covered embankment. I came out behind a 7-Eleven.

I hadn't made it a few yards down the road when I saw another group of skinheads in the distance. I didn't recognize them as anyone that I knew. I figured they were up for the rally. They were crowded around something on the ground. As they pulled back I saw it. If I hadn't been there I wouldn't have believed it. One of them was finishing assaulting a person on the street with a hammer. The others jeered and kicked the victim who was motionless.

I wanted to scream but found myself frozen with shock. Unable to believe what I had witnessed, horror turned into fear and my pulse began to race. Ducking down between cars and scrambling across the ground, I stayed low so they wouldn't see me. It wasn't as though they would have attacked me. I was one of them, at least if they went by appearances, but they were strangers and they might not have been as lenient as Bryan Catz was. I peered over the trunk of a car. They'd moved on from the victim. He was no longer moving. A puddle of blood pooled around his head. They strolled up the high street singing punk songs as though they had done no wrong.

I sure as hell didn't sign up for that. Moving quickly out of the parking lot and over to Pearl Street, I found house 483. Peering around nervously, I banged on the door and someone peered out of the curtain. I heard a chain slide across, multiple locks pull back and then it opened.

Jodi immediately grabbed me and held me tight.

"You're back?"

"Yeah. Yeah." I looked around panting and breathing hard. I was in the hallway of the Robertsons'. I'd only met them a few times when Jodi had invited them over for supper. They were your typical family. Bill and Rachel Robertson had two small children under the age of nine. Apparently Jodi knew them from way back in the day when she used to go to school with Rachel.

"Have you seen what it's like out there?" I said thumbing over my shoulder.

"No. We've been here since the power went out. Bill has a generator."

I glanced at the lights that were on.

"Turn them off."

"What?"

"Turn off the lights." I began rushing around flipping them off. "If they see them on they will show up here."

"Who will? Sam, you are scaring me."

As I hurried to shut off the lights, Brett stopped me.

"Son, what's going on?"

I was still breathing hard from running. The image of the guy getting his head smashed in with a hammer was stuck in my mind. The words of Bryan Catz rang in my ears. It all seemed surreal.

"Do you need a drink?"

"I'll get him a drink."

"No. I'm serious. You've got to turn these lights out."

Bill Robertson got up from his seat and stood in front of me. "You are scaring my children, Sam. Stop."

"Do any of you know what has happened?"

Brett came closer. "Yeah, there was talk of terrorist attacks before the blackout. Several cities have been hit with explosives or something like that."

"It's a nuclear attack."

"What are you on about?" Brett's brow knit together.

I ran my hand over my stubbled head.

"You know the group that I was hanging out with

before I went away? They are part of a larger network. White supremacists. A massive organization that is spread across the United States. Whoever runs that organization must have had some strong connections as they are the ones responsible for this. Now by the looks of it, the explosions were only the beginning. In nearly every city and state of America they are gearing up to take control of what remains of towns and cities that haven't been affected by the strikes."

"Nuclear strikes? How?"

"Suitcase bombs. I'd heard them talking about it but I just thought it was, you know... a joke. In the Cold War—"

I was in mid-sentence when the window smashed. A large rock missed Bill's face by inches and came to rest near my feet. It was followed by someone shouting.

"Come on out."

"Shit. They're here." They had seen the lights on in the house. It was only a matter of time before the chaos kicked off. With zero power they would be looking for anyone who was running a generator.

"What the hell is going on?" Bill was a large man and not the kind of guy that would have been intimidated by anyone. When another rock came through the window and hit his daughter in the back, he was beyond pissed.

"Little fuckers." He stormed towards the front door.

"No. Don't open that."

I rushed forward but it was too late. The second the door swung wide, another brick came flying and hit him full force in the face. Bill fell back on the ground, his face a bloody mess. Outside, there was jeering and shouts.

"Lock the door," I screamed.

Brett scrambled to the door and shouldered it like an NFL player. I dragged out an armchair and rammed it against the door, then returned to the living room. Rachel was screaming. Her kids were crying. Staying low to the ground I approached an open window. I shouted to the guys outside.

"Back off. I'm dealing with this."

There were a few seconds before they replied. "Sam?"

I recognized the voice as Tommy Black. He'd been one of two people who had initially got me involved in the group. He was a good guy, at least he appeared that way to me.

"Tommy. I'm handling this."

"What the fuck are you doing in there, Frost?" another voice shouted. I peered out through the thin white drapes.

Markus Wainright stood outside with Tommy and three other skinheads I didn't know. I'd met him on a number of occasions. He was considered a leader among our group. The group that ran out of Mount Pleasant consisted of about thirty individuals of varying ages. There had been talks of a rally being held months ago. I just thought they were talking shit. Back then very little had been shared with us. We were considered foot soldiers. Whatever the hell that meant. All we had been told was to get ready for something big. It was going to be a landmark for white supremacists everywhere. They had said it would make Middle Eastern terrorist attacks look like child's play. I thought they were kidding.

All of them were armed with baseball bats, thick two-by-fours and large knives. That was one thing about the group. They were into inflicting pain, not just shooting people. In the distance behind them I could see even more taking to the streets. Large flashlights were being shone around the streets and anyone who was out was attacked. Several kicked in doors that had lights on. Others tossed Molotov cocktails and set cars on fire.

"Just leave it with me," I hollered.

"The hell I will. That isn't your house."

"Give me a minute."

I looked over my shoulder to Brett. I indicated for him to go out the back. He shook his head. He was stubborn.

The heated conversation came back to me in that moment. My mind drifted to the day before being hauled away to Camp Zero.

Brett followed me into my room and closed the door. I had never seen him angry. His approach was very different to other foster parents I had. The previous wouldn't think twice about taking out a belt and unleashing hell on my rear end. I still had the scars to prove it.

No, Brett was smart. He got inside my head and used reverse psychology. He believed that my problem was a lack of love, and that any time someone showed care, I shut down or had a violent outburst.

He wasn't wrong. Then again, he hadn't spent the last years being bounced around from family to family.

I was packing a bag when he came in. Lt. Scot Murphy was in the other room with Dan. It was like an intervention for a drug user. They had shown up and were planning on taking me in. They had given me the option to go pack a few things and leave with them quietly or they would take me by force. At first I thought it was joke, some kind of prank, but they were dead serious.

Of course I didn't plan on sticking around so I ran into my room and started stuffing a duffel bag with some of my personal belongings.

That's when Brett entered.

"Sam, we are trying to help. This isn't you. The shaved

head, the tattoo, the swastika on the wall. It's all just a front."

"Oh yeah, what the fuck do you know?"

"I know that beneath all that, you just want someone to actually give a shit about you."

I looked back at him blankly.

"I know that you have been through hell with previous foster parents but we aren't like that."

"You know how many times I've heard that?"

"It's true."

"Oh, and you think sending me away to some shithole in the middle of the wilderness is going to fix me?"

"These guys know what they are doing. They have worked with hundreds of kids just like you."

I slammed my bag down and got up in his face. "Just like me? What am I, some freak of nature to you?" I paused staring into his dark eyes. "Why did you choose me? Why not a black kid?"

"Do you think the color of your skin matters to us?"

"Well, doesn't it?"

He never backed down. He remained poised and looked into my eyes. "Son."

"I'm not your son. I'm your paycheck."

"You're not a paycheck, Sam."

I turned away and continued stuffing clothes into my bag.

"Sam."

As he grabbed hold of my arm and spun me around, I nearly said a word that I had never uttered before. I didn't even know where it came from. In the heat of the moment it nearly came out.

"Get off me you…" I paused in mid-sentence. It was then that I realized that I had overstepped a line.

"Go on. Say it."

"Screw you, Brett."

I pushed past him with my bag, and slammed the door open. Jodi had tears in her eyes. I had nearly made it to the door when Murphy stepped in front of me.

"I guess we have to do this the hard way."

Another rock came through the window sending

shards of glass across the room. I knew if they came in they would kill Jodi and Brett and no doubt myself included. I scrambled across the floor.

"You need to get out of here. Head to City Hall, Murphy will be there." I glanced up at the clock, it was a little after six thirty. If nothing had happened to him he would be there.

Brett screwed up his face. "I'm not leaving you here."

"They won't touch me. They see me as one of them."

"But you're not."

I hesitated before I replied. "I know. Just go."

Brett clasped Jodi's hand and led her out the back door. Bill's face was covered in blood; Rachel held a towel to it. I felt bad for the guy. Both of their children were crying and looked terrified. Once I saw they had safely made it out back I went into the kitchen and looked around for anything that I could use to defend myself. There was a knife rack on the counter. I grabbed the largest one and tucked it into the back of my jeans.

"You better bring them out now, Frost, or we're

coming in."

What I did next was probably the most idiotic thing I could have done. I went over to the wall and smashed the side of my head against it twice until it created a cut above my eye and blood began to trickle down. I staggered over to the front door and began pulling the armchair back just as they began to smash against it with bats.

"Hold on, I'm opening up."

I dragged the chair away from the front door, yanked it open then fell back on the ground as though I was struggling to catch my breath. The first person I came face-to-face with was Markus.

"What the hell happened to you?"

"They overpowered me."

"Where are the others?"

"It was just me. I thought I would do this one myself. I saw the light and thought we could use the generator."

"You fucking idiot." Markus pushed me out of the way.

"Where did they go?"

"Out the back. They're long gone."

"Not for long they won't. We are all over this town now. Right, guys, grab whatever you can and haul that generator out of here." He then proceeded to smash everything in sight with a bat that had nails coming out of it. Photo frames that held memories scattered across the room. One of them brought in a small red gasoline can and started splashing the walls and furniture.

"That's it. Soak it real good. Without any power we are going to need some light, especially if we have to track these little rats down."

By rats he was referring to anyone who wasn't a skinhead. It was a term they had used multiple times in the past.

Right then Tommy Black came in. He was a heavyset guy with tattoos all over his arms and body modifications that made him look as though he had horns under his skin.

"When did you get back?"

"Tonight."

"Gotta love your timing." He grabbed a hold of my hand and hauled me up off the ground and then passed me a cloth from the kitchen. "Stick that on your face, Frost. That is a gnarly cut. Did those bastards do it?"

I nodded, holding a hand up to my head.

"Don't worry, they'll pay. Everyone is going to pay today. I fucking love it."

With that said he stuck his iPhone earbuds into his ears and began going nuts on the place with a baseball bat. I watched as they desecrated the home, ripping up furniture and smashing holes in the walls. One of them took a piss up the wall and then Markus gestured for everyone to get out. At which point he flicked open a Zippo lighter. The flame danced in the air right before he tossed it into the house.

A sudden gust of fire and the entire place was engulfed in flames.

CITY HALL

Stuck with a bunch of raving lunatics, I didn't imagine it could get any worse. I was wrong. Occasionally I glanced back over my shoulder at the fiery house that was now engulfed. My mind was preoccupied with thoughts of Jodi and Brett's safety. I needed to get to City Hall.

"What's going on?" I asked.

"No one told you?"

"Yeah, something about a rally and whatnot but to be honest I didn't think they were going to go this far."

Markus let out a laugh. He was eyeing the different houses looking for any that were lit up by generators. Two of the men were lugging the other generator between them.

"It's a new world now, my friend," Tommy said becoming all theatrical. "Picture in your mind small towns all over the country. I mean, the ones that haven't been obliterated by the blast or affected by the nuclear

JACK HUNT

fallout. Picture them under our control. This country is finally going to be run the right way."

By our kind he meant anyone who was a neo-Nazi, white supremacist.

"But what about your family?"

His eyes drifted down for a second. "This is my family."

I could tell he didn't believe that. But fear was a strong motivator. Sure, people could run but at this point I didn't think the townsfolk truly knew what was taking place. We were shrouded in darkness and the only light came from people's flashlights or houses that were on fire. There was no point in me telling them that I had to get back to my family, they would have laughed. All of them had been egging me on for close to a year to do my foster parents in. Initially that was meant to be how I would earn my red laces. I wouldn't do it. It wasn't that I cared for them at that point. I had only been with them a year but I could tell they were good people. They weren't like the others I had been with. Not that all the families I had

82

been placed in were bad. In many ways I was the one that had kept them at arm's length. But there had been a few nasty assholes.

Instead, they had taken me over to a different town and had me beat a kid within an inch of his life. I didn't even know who he was. His face still haunted me. Had he survived the beating? For months after, I had expected the police to show up at the door and arrest me. I had even considered handing myself in and admitting to it. The irony was, the kid wasn't black, he wasn't Jewish, he wasn't anything that might have been taken as racial. He'd pissed off some guy in our group by posting a video online of a crime. It seems the skinhead in the video had taken a firework and attached it to a cat's tail and lit it. I wasn't there for the actual thing but I saw the video. It was horrible. That was the beginning of when I knew I had fallen in with the wrong crowd but by then I was entrenched. At first I tried to justify it in my mind as a few bad apples in the group. I never imagined it would escalate to what I was seeing now.

I looked in the direction of where the others were pointing their flashlights. Occasionally the sound of screams filled the air. A few of them laughed. They fucking laughed at someone else's demise. I regretted ever meeting Tommy.

"Where are we going?"

"To the rally. It's being held down on Main Street."

As we walked along the residential streets others joined us. There had to have been at least thirty other skinheads. All of them armed, some covered in blood. I saw a couple of handguns stashed inside the front of waistbands. As we rounded a corner, a short distance away police officers were handcuffing two skinheads. The moment the others saw it they broke into a run like a bunch of soccer hooligans. The look on the faces of the officers was pure fear. They knew what was coming. I knew it was now or never. I broke away from the group into an overgrown trail that ran down the side of a block of houses. That was the thing about Mount Pleasant. The entire town had been built inside a large forest. On either side of the valley were mountains that overshadowed us. Steep slopes were covered in a vast ocean of green. Pine trees for as far as the eye could see. There were only two ways in and out of the town; one on the east and another on the west side. With the town bordering I-90 it would have been very easy for them to block off the major roads so no one could escape by vehicle.

Right now all I could think about was getting away. I heard my name called but I didn't respond or look back. I had to hope that the police had caused a big enough distraction that no one would follow. In the darkness I tripped and landed hard against the ground. A shot of pain went through my knee as I pushed myself back up on my feet and kept running. I climbed over four fences and saw several dead bodies on my way to City Hall. City Hall was located on the far east side of the town right beside the local police and fire department. A large red brick and mortar building, with multiple offices inside, it was a hub of activity by day.

I had made it around one of the corners when I

crashed into someone on a bicycle. I didn't see who they were until I was on the ground groaning in agony. The wheel had hit me right between the nuts.

"Look where you're going."

I looked up and that's when both of us locked eyes. It was Billy Manning. Tangled up in his bike chain, he looked as nervous as hell.

"Billy?"

"Sam?"

I groaned and staggered to my feet, trying to help him up. It took a minute or two to get his pant leg untangled from the chain. It was covered in oil. Once we brushed ourselves off, I pulled the bike into a thicket of trees so that we'd be out of sight.

"You know what the hell's going on? I just saw somebody get stabbed to death two doors down from me. I was on my way down to Mick's bar to see if my old man was there."

"You don't want to go that way. I'm heading to City Hall."

"To meet Murphy? Are you out of your mind, we just spent a month with that fool. I'm not —"

I grabbed a hold of him. "Do you want to end up dead?"

He chuckled prying my grip from his shirt. "What? You and whose army?"

I gestured with my head down the street to a pack of skinheads who were making their way up.

"Okay, what did you have in mind?" And just like that he changed his tune. We dashed into the forest. We were at least ten blocks from City Hall and there was no way in hell we were going to be able to make it there by sticking to the roads. The skinheads were all over the place.

"You want to tell me what is going on?" Billy demanded to know.

"Just shut the hell up and keep moving."

"I swear I knew it would come to this. Every one is fucking mad in this town. Oh shit, do you think this is some kind of disease that makes everyone shave their heads?"

I rolled my eyes at his stupidity as he continued droning on.

"I tell you it's just typical. We get sent away to that shithole for a month and all hell breaks loose back in our town. And yet I bet they still think we are the ones with issues."

As I did my best to ignore his verbal diarrhea, we pushed on through the thick undergrowth towards a light in the distance.

Billy grabbed my jacket and thumbed into the forest.

"Why don't we just get out of here?"

"And go where? Go if you want to, I'm heading to City Hall. Brett and Jodi are there. Besides, Murphy might know what to do."

We stayed close to the town, just inside the tree line. It took us the better part of twenty minutes to make it to the rear of City Hall. When it was in sight, we crouched at the edge of the forest casting our eyes up and down the street to make sure that it was clear before we made a move. When we burst out of the bushes, we didn't stop running until we reached the back door. It was locked of course, so we began banging. I glanced around thinking that at any minute now the noise was going to attract them. Fear ran through me at the thought of a cluster of skinheads showing up.

"Let's try around front," Billy said hopping down off the five steps that led up to the back door. Just as he made it a few feet away, the door cracked open. It was Murphy. I'd never felt so relieved to see him as I did in that moment.

"Guys."

We bolted inside and he slammed the door behind us.

"You guys okay?" He pointed to my head and I just waved him off. Murphy led us into a spacious office area where everyone was. Corey and Luke were already there. There were about sixteen other people filling up the corridor as well as a few rooms. Most were folks I recognized from around town. Mainly adults in their forties and fifties. Certainly not the kind of people that would have been ready to deal with this. Hell, none of us were prepared for this.

"Where are Jodi and Brett?"

"Were they supposed to be here?"

My brow knit together. "I told them to go here."

"Perhaps they stopped somewhere. I'm surprised you are even here, Frost. I thought you would be outside with all your crazy buddies," Luke sneered at me as he paced back and forth. He had a cigarette in the corner of his mouth. I didn't reply.

Right then Ally Murphy came in from the corridor. Her mother Sara was close behind her, and some other guy who I figured was her new boyfriend.

Ally glanced at me and looked up and down.

"Is there enough diesel for the generator?" Murphy asked.

His daughter replied. "There are a few cans down there but not a lot. Maybe a couple of days' worth if we are lucky." She looked at me again. Murphy caught me looking. "Ally, this is…"

"I know. I've seen him around school."

I quickly shifted the attention away from myself.

"What about your family, Corey?" I asked then noticing he had blood on his hands.

"My mother and sister are out back." He held up his bloodied knuckles. "I had to take out two guys on the way. They just started attacking us. I don't even know why."

"I do."

Their eyes fell upon me. I quickly brought them up to speed on what had happened so far. What I had been told and what it seemed was going on around the country.

Murphy immediately went into defense mode. "I need to get to my house. Grab some weapons."

"Weapons? You planning on starting a war?" Sara asked.

"Look around you, Sara. It's already begun. This isn't going to get any better. You heard yourself. They are already taking out the police."

I thought back to the two police officers. I didn't even want to think about what had happened to them.

"Has anyone checked the station next door for weapons?" I asked.

Murphy replied. "Already done. It's locked up tight because of the riot. We'd need to find one of the officers."

"No, no. I say we get the hell out of town now while we can," Luke said.

Edgar Wheeler who owned a gas station on the outskirts of town spoke up. He was chewing a piece of tobacco in the side of his mouth and spitting black gunk into a small can beside him.

"There's no leaving except by foot. They have already blocked off the main road on the east side. Even then, I highly doubt you are going to last long out there." He looked at me. "If you say they are doing this in some of the other towns, we are screwed either way."

"So we ride it out," an elderly lady in her mid sixties spoke up. I had seen her around town but I didn't know her. "We can hide here."

"They'll find you," I muttered. "This is just the beginning."

"Where are they doing?" Corey asked.

"There's a rally being held down on Main Street. But I don't think they are planning on staying there. I think they are just gathering everyone together and then the real anarchy will start."

"Hell, it's already begun," someone else muttered.

Some older women walked into the room. The moment their eyes locked on me I could see the fear. "What's he doing here? He's one of them."

Four guys who worked for the local lumberyard must have overheard them as they came rushing into the room pointing towards the back door. "Get him out."

"Now just hold up," Murphy said putting his arm between them and me.

"What are you doing? He'll bring 'em this way."

One guy tried to go for me and Murphy pushed him back. "Back off."

The air was thick. Everyone's eyes were on me.

"He's not one of them," Murphy said before looking at me. I had to wonder if that was truly what he believed.

I didn't reply as it didn't matter what I said; the others wouldn't have believed me.

"You're telling us he's not one of them? Look at him."

The green bomber jacket and black Doc Martens weren't exactly helping. Had I known before I left the house, I would have chosen something else. It was just force of habit.

"Why is he even in here?"

"Because he's my son."

I turned around to see Brett. "You made it."

They came into the room breathing hard. Alongside him were Jodi, the Robertsons and their daughters. Directly behind them was an injured police officer. He stumbled into the room with a wound in his side. Several other men tried to support him. Sara who was a nurse immediately went to work on trying to help. One of the women disappeared and returned with some towels.

"I thought you hadn't made it," I said to Brett.

"We nearly didn't. If it wasn't for him," he motioned to the officer, "we all would have been killed. Of that I'm sure." The officer looked up from the table. Sara tore open his uniform. There were two knife wounds in the lower part of his stomach. He was bleeding out fast.

"Go to the front desk. There should be a first-aid kit in the third drawer down," she muttered. The officer's gold badge on his chest had the name Ridgewood etched into it. I knew I recognized him. He was one of the main officers who had pulled me in on misdemeanor charges. He was in his late twenties. Built extremely well, he almost looked like he was stitched into his uniform.

A few minutes passed and one of the women returned with a first-aid kit. She glanced at me again and kept her distance. Sara went to work on dressing the abdominal wound.

"Not even the shortwave radio is working."

"I have Dan's CB and two sets of two-way ham radios at my place," Murphy said. "I need to get to it and make contact with him."

"And what? Is he going to bring the cavalry? For all we know he's already dead."

Murphy must have found that humorous. The guy had lived his entire life in the military. This must have seemed like a walk in the park to him. When all of us were falling apart at the seams in the wilderness he looked as if he was in his element.

"Wouldn't that have been affected by the EMP?"

"No, Dan was big on keeping those protected. It's stored in a small Faraday cage."

Murphy was assisting Sara. I noticed the guy who came in with Sara looked at Murphy. There was some definite animosity there.

"Should I even bother asking what that is?" Brett asked.

Murphy didn't reply immediately.

"It's a means of protection from electrostatic and electromagnetic interference."

"What the hell, was Dan expecting this to happen?"

He glanced over at everyone who was watching him and for a brief second smirked. "You obviously don't know Dan very well. The guy expects everything to happen. Now don't stand there gawking. Barricade the doors with anything you can find."

"And then what?" one of the older women asked.

"I kind of have my hands tied right now," he said, covered in blood from helping Sara.

"What about the windows?"

"What about them?"

"They are setting fire to business buildings."

City Hall was made of brick but it wouldn't have stopped them throwing Molotov cocktails through the glass windows. We would die from smoke inhalation. The moment we stepped outside they would hack us to death.

Murphy with a dead serious face just pointed to the doors. "Go and do as I've asked."

Everyone start grabbing chairs, tables, anything they could find and dragging them into the hallway. We began stacking them up in front of the main doors which were just glass and steel. It wouldn't take them long to put two and two together and see that all that shit was there to protect those inside. City Hall was attached to the police station. One of the older women mentioned making a hole in the wall through to the station so that we could expand it and create an escape route. But that idea vanished when the officer said that there was a two-foot thick brick wall between the two buildings.

Once the doors were barricaded, some of the oldies started looking for anything that could be used as a weapon. In City Hall there was nothing except office furniture. Some of them broke off pieces of wood from chair legs and wrapped up shards of glass in towels.

The guys from the lumberyard paced back and forth.

"I don't like this. I say we move now, while they are still gathering. We could get out of town through the forest."

"What do you say?" They posed the question to Murphy who was still helping the wounded officer.

"No, we need to stick together," Brett said.

"We will. But leaving on foot."

Sara spoke up. "This man is too injured. He can't and I'm not leaving him."

"That's not our problem," one of the men spat back. "I'm not losing my life over one man."

Murphy spun around.

"You want to leave. Go now. No one is stopping you. But we are staying to help."

A few of their wives began to cry as they told them to get moving. Fear had taken hold as the harsh reality bore down on us all. People would divide as the fight-or-flight instinct kicked in. Edgar was right, even if we could hike out, we wouldn't survive long. We had zero food, no protection from the elements and currently no weapons. The harsh mountainous terrain would have kicked our asses long before we had managed to get to safety.

In many ways leaving would have been like an extreme version of Camp Zero.

"No, he's right, Murphy. A few of us are going to have to venture out. It won't be long before they make their way down here. If there are over two hundred of them, those doors are not going to hold," Bill Robertson said, still sporting a terrible bloodied gash on his face. "I have kids to think about. C'mon, Rachel. Hey! Hold up," he shouted to the lumber guys who were in the processing of removing what we had stacked on twenty minutes earlier.

"Where do you live, Murphy?" Edgar asked.

"On the west side."

"Shit."

The thought of trying to make it across town with groups of skinheads searching for survivors only added to the anxiety we felt.

"I have a home on the edge of town."

"Let me guess, you are one of those prepper types with everything stored up?" Corey asked.

"Actually no, that's Dan. I have weapons. Beyond that I have stocked up on a few things mainly because Dan badgered me but no, I wish I did."

"What about the fallout? Radiation and shit like that? Shouldn't we be down in some bunker or something?" Luke asked. "I've heard that if you don't die from the blast, you can die from radiation?"

Murphy didn't reply. I don't think it was because he

didn't know. I think there was little he could do. There was little any of us could do.

"You don't think they would set one off in this town, do you?" Billy asked.

"I highly doubt it, they want control of this town. Bryan Catz had mentioned the organization had targeted the grid and military installations. I imagine they hit New York, Los Angeles, maybe Washington and some of the larger cities, leaving enough left over for them to control and start again. We're not talking about a missile here, guys. These are one kiloton. It's still a lot of power but the particles from the blast would mostly land in areas where people had already been killed."

"But the weather can affect it. I mean, it could blow some of those particles for miles."

Murphy nodded.

"This is fucked up," Corey said getting up and walking back and forth.

"Take a seat, big man," Billy said. "We only have so much air in here, and you are sucking most of it up."

Corey scowled at him, balling his fists. He might have floored him in the wilderness but right now it wouldn't have done him much good. We had bigger issues to deal with.

"Who's going to come with me?" Murphy asked.

"I'll go."

Murphy paused for a few seconds then looked around.

"Has anyone seen Kate?"

DEGENERATES

Murphy's home was close to Mount Pleasant Inn. It was a good fifteen-minute walk on an ordinary day but with the streets filled with lunatics it was liable to take us close to thirty, maybe more. No one wanted to step a foot outside the doors and we weren't going to take the chance of losing Murphy.

We pulled together anything that could be considered a weapon in a pile on the table. It was a pitiful sight. There were a few pieces of wood, a couple of butter knives, several shards of glass and a large wrench that belonged to Edgar. Besides that Murphy was carrying a Glock, and I had a carving knife from my house. It wasn't exactly instilling confidence in us.

"Scot, are you sure about this?" Sara asked.

"We don't have any other choice. If I don't get over to my house, we aren't going to have the means to protect ourselves. Listen, I'm going to leave the Glock with you."

"Are you out of your mind?" Edgar said. "We are going to need it out there."

"No, I want to make sure that if anyone comes through those doors other than the police, or someone needing help, they have some way to protect themselves."

"I'm coming with you," Ally said.

"No, sweetheart, you're staying here."

"Matt," Murphy handed him the Glock. "Look after them."

Ally began to protest. "Dad, I'm not staying here."

"It's too dangerous, Ally."

"Oh, but it's okay for you and them?" She pointed at me.

He shook his head and Matt tried to intervene.

"Ally. Listen to him."

She put up a hand without even looking at him. "You're not my father, Matt."

I saw Murphy's eyes dart between them. A look of concern, perhaps amusement crossed his face. It couldn't have been easy seeing someone else living with your ex.

"You think he's going to be okay?" Corey enquired about the cop who was out cold on the table.

"He's lost a lot of blood. He really needs to get to a hospital soon," Sara replied.

Murphy went to take the wrench and Edgar placed his meaty hand on it. "I'm coming with you and that's mine."

"Fair enough." He reached for what appeared to be a wooden chair leg. He slapped it in his other hand a few times as if testing how strong it was. All I could think about was how many skinheads were out there and how they had smashed in some guy's face with a hammer.

It was decided that Luke, Edgar and myself would go. We didn't want too many people out there. Corey and Billy would stay to offer additional help just in case anything went south.

"Stay quiet. Keep the lights off and we'll be back soon," Murphy said before giving his daughter a kiss on the forehead.

After being in the wilderness for the past month we

had pretty much been schooled in the means of being creative. If we didn't get creative we didn't sleep or eat. It was as simple as that. Matt offered Murphy a large flashlight but he declined.

"That'll only attract attention. By the way, turn off the generator. They are focusing in on homes and companies that have generators. Those will be the first places they hit."

"I'll go do that," Jim Emerson, owner of a local bar and grill, disappeared off down the hall.

Murphy walked back over to Matt. "Only use the gun if they get through those doors. Unless they break in, don't fire. We'll knock three times when we get back so you know it's us."

Ally hugged her father one more time and we moved out. At the back of the building we began pulling the chairs away. Matt and a few of the other men got ready to block it the second we got outside. As the door cracked open my heart started beating faster. Murphy was the first out. Except for the glow of fires in the distance it was pitch-black outside. Staying together in one line we moved with purpose across the parking lot keeping ourselves low to the ground. The lot came out on Cedar Street and shoehorned around an elementary school. So far we hadn't seen anyone except a couple of locals who still seemed to be oblivious to what was taking place in the town. Murphy tried to warn them but they just thought we were insane and darted across the street away from us. It probably didn't help that we were creeping along holding a wrench, a knife and two chair legs.

Murphy shook his head looking over at them before Edgar spoke.

"There's no time. We just need to get there."

He nodded and we pressed on, circling the school. Cedar crossed over Sixth Street, went past the Oasis Museum and several fish restaurants. We hung a right on Sixth Street and double-timed it north. We remained in the shadows, ducking into alleyways every time we heard movement.

"You think they are all on Main Street?" Edgar asked.

"That's where they said they were heading. Down to the large church building."

We had made it as far as the Northern Pacific Depot Railroad Museum. High above us was I-90 that passed overhead. The initial goal was to go underneath it and head into the forest just beyond but that would not happen. They had blocked off the road with multiple vehicles and up ahead were six skinheads keeping watch. One of them had a chain in his hand and was swinging it around while the others were raiding Alibi's Steakhouse. They had taken a large metal trashcan and thrown it through the front window. Several of them were inside. We could only see six from where we were but we were sure there were more.

"Okay, change of plan. We are going down Pine Street."

"But that's going to bring us out close to Main Street."

"Not if we hang a left four blocks down and go north on Front."

Luke let out a chuckle. "If we can make it there."

"It's a straight run."

"Yeah, straight past those baldies over there."

Murphy leaned back against a wall close to a large industrial dumpster.

"The alternative is we head back and go west on Cedar Street," Edgar said.

"Which will bring you directly into Main Street," I added. "No, listen up, I know what to do. Just hang back here."

"What?" Murphy said in a hushed tone.

Before I could explain or he could stop me, I tucked the knife into the back of my jeans and darted out between two vehicles. I began rushing in the direction of the six skinheads.

"Oy! Cops are heading for Main Street." I didn't wait to see if they would follow, I just kept running. With my green bomber jacket on, my jeans and trimmed hair, they didn't think twice. They just assumed I was one of them and began running to catch up with me. I turned back momentarily. Now that the skinheads were facing the other direction, the others were able to get across the street without being seen. I slowed down and placed my hands on my knees pretending to be out of breath. They shot by me, only one of them turned back to ask if I was okay. I waved him on and watched them disappear around a corner. Looking back, I could see Murphy and the others were already halfway down the street. They hugged the sides of the buildings. Just three dark silhouettes moving unnoticed through the night.

We had started heading up Fifth Street, which would eventually merge into Front, when our luck went out the window. For a brief while we thought the darkness would keep us from being spotted, we were wrong. As we passed by River Street a set of headlights flicked on lighting us up. They were the super-bright halogen kind, the ones that blind even if you shield your eyes in time. As the lights flicked off, I blinked hard allowing my vision to adjust. That's when I saw them. There had to have been at least eight with bats, chains and knives.

For what seemed like a minute or two, but was likely

only a few seconds, we stared back.

"Holy shit," Luke muttered before we made a break for it. The sound of hollering and boots pounding asphalt behind us was enough to make my blood run cold.

"Go, go, go." I don't know why I was saying it, as the others were running as fast as they could. I cast a glance over my shoulder to see them catching up.

"I'm thinking we could have used that Glock about now," Edgar hollered.

Mount Pleasant Library was the closest building to us. Fifteen large concrete steps led up to a set of dark brown wood doors. Murphy smashed his foot against one but it didn't give way.

He tried again but it was too late. On the ground the skinheads prowled around the lower steps looking devilish.

"Stay the fuck back!" Luke said swiping the air with a thick chair leg.

"Brave, are we?" One of them stepped forward slapping his baseball bat in his hand in a taunting manner. I had seen him before. He was one of the skinheads being handcuffed by the two officers earlier. My eyes scanned the rest of their faces, hoping to see at least one member that I knew. They were all from out of town.

"And look at this fucker," he pointed his bat towards me. "What are you doing running with them?"

"Look, man, we don't want no trouble."

He cocked his head and got this grin.

"A shit-eating turncoat," another one said.

That was the extent of the conversation. The guy gestured with his finger and the others rushed the stairs. Four against eight wasn't exactly good odds but then again they didn't have someone who was a SEAL, or a mechanic who looked as if he had swung that wrench a few times.

As a chain wrapped itself around my one leg, I kicked a guy in the face with the other and he fell back down the stairs into two others like dominoes collapsing. We had the advantage of high ground. The fifteen steps were steep and there was only one way they could get at us and that was by coming up. Murphy obviously didn't see it that way as he hopped over the side down onto the green in an attempt to draw a couple of them away. I might have enjoyed seeing him go ape shit on the two guys but I was in the process of unwrapping the thick chain from my leg. I turned to see Edgar bring his wrench down on one guy's skull so hard, it caved in. A spray of red mist hit my face as the skinhead dropped making it harder for the next guy behind him to get up the steps. Luke wielded a wooden chair leg like it was Thor's axe, clobbering one skinhead so hard around the face that I was sure he had killed the guy. I didn't even have a chance to get that chain off before another was up and on me. He knocked me back towards the ground and was trying to force a machete down on my face. With my back pressed against the concrete I felt the carving knife in my waistband dig into my flesh. There was no way I could get at it as the guy above me was using his full body weight to try and push this sideways blade down on my face. It felt like I was bench pressing two people at the same time. If it hadn't been for Luke kicking the guy in the gut, I was pretty sure he would have jammed that blade through my skull. The very second the guy fell off, I reached around, pulled the knife and jammed it into his leg. He let out a high-pitched scream and staggered back. Meanwhile Edgar was still going nuts with his oversized wrench. I noticed he had been cut as he was bleeding from his side but it wasn't stopping him. Reaching down to my leg, I pulled off the chain, wrapped it around my fist so a large piece dangled down and then unleashed it like a whip around the face of the guy who was climbing the stairs with a spiked knuckleduster.

He let out a blood-curdling scream before Murphy came up behind him and slit his throat.

We all stood there for a second gazing at the bloody aftermath. My hand was shaking.

Now I don't think we got lucky, we just wanted to live more than they did. As I looked around at the carnage, those that were still alive were groaning on the floor, writing around in pain. Panting hard, I pulled the knife from the guy's leg and he let out another cry. At least he wasn't dead. I wasn't sure I was ready to kill anyone.

Murphy wiped a bloody knife on his leg.

We grabbed up what weapons they were carrying and set off again.

Front Street was on the far edge of town. We could hear the noise of people screaming along with laughter and chaos erupting in the streets. What little calm remained after the blackout was now gone. Anarchy was alive in the streets like a snake seeking to devour and destroy.

"How much longer?" Edgar asked.

"A few more blocks," Murphy replied with a stoic look on his face. We were getting close to Third Street and Cypress when we saw another group. They had dragged out several people from an inn and were beating them. A woman pleaded for her husband's life but they didn't care. They were savages.

I wanted to help but there were too many of them and

Murphy told us to keep moving. We might have escaped death back at the library but the chance of being able to fend off another attack was unlikely, especially when there were only four us and at least fifteen of them.

The journey to Murphy's place was tough but it was only made harder by the constant stopping and starting. We had to drop down behind cars, and behind fences. All the while we had a front seat to the torture of human life. They were like a pack of rabid wolves encircling their prey and taking turns to inflict as much as harm as possible.

In a town with a population of just over eight hundred, it wouldn't be long before they would overtake and control the streets. It wasn't even like the police could radio for help. This was a sudden and coordinated attack. Like a lion waiting in the undergrowth, just biding its time, waiting for the right moment to pounce.

We eventually arrived at Murphy's place. It wasn't anything fancy. Just a small clapboard house set back from the road, shrouded by trees with a small gravel driveway that led up to a property that couldn't have been more than fifteen hundred square foot.

"Didn't you come here first?" Luke asked.

"No, I went straight to City Hall after collecting Sara from the hospital and picking up Ally and Matt."

As we made our way in, Luke carried on peppering him with questions. "So what's the deal with him? When did your ex meet Matt?"

"She's not my ex. Well, she is but not on paper. We haven't finalized the divorce."

"How long have you been separated?"

He unlocked a metal cabinet inside his house and pulled out an M4 carbine, along with two AR-15s.

"Here, hold this."

I stared down at it.

"Isn't that illegal?" Edgar asked.

Murphy just rolled his eyes. He was obviously used to hearing all manner of questions about weapons and what was or wasn't allowed in the country. He didn't even bother to answer.

"What kind of firepower does this put out?" I asked. I

had seen and fired a Remington rifle but nothing like these two.

"The Colt M4 Carbine, 700 rounds per minute. The AR-15 is 30 rounds every fifteen seconds."

Murphy then disappeared into another room. I looked at Edgar. Luke was staring out the window, making sure that no one was coming. When Murphy reappeared he had what looked like two large briefcases in his hands. He set them down against the wall and then went into the kitchen. I shuffled over and peered in. He opened the fridge, it was dark inside. He pulled out a bottle of beer, popped the cap off with a twist and chugged it down in one hit. As he closed the fridge, I could see he had several photos of his daughter Ally tacked against it using fridge magnets. There was a sign on the wall with the words: *The only easy day was yesterday.*

I'd always been fascinated by anyone that had gone into the military and was willing to put their life on the line for their country. Besides cops, I didn't think there was anything more courageous than laying down your life down for another. Though there was a mystique surrounding the teams. SEALs weren't superhuman but they were the closest we had to guys who knew how to live and work in the most uncomfortable environments. They had the mindset, the skillset and drive to survive when others would want to roll over and die.

"Murphy. Do you think those guys got away?"

"Who?"

"Robertson and the men from the lumberyard?"

"Who knows?"

"After what we just went through I'm thinking they were smart to leave," Luke muttered.

He was at it again. I didn't blame him. Logically, hiding in the woods or making a run for it made sense. But he wasn't seeing the bigger picture. We had no idea if they had escaped, or the full extent of what the country was going through.

"And go where? The chances of us being able to survive out there are slim. We don't know where those bombs went off or how far the fallout has spread but we know it can't be anywhere near here otherwise these idiots wouldn't be sticking around. So my guess is this place is a safe zone for now. Besides, it's home and I damn well am not going to sit back and watch a bunch of knucklehead baldies fuck up my town."

"You said Dan had a bunker."

Murphy slammed a magazine into the M4.

"That he does."

"Hey, I'm all for raising a little hell but there are a lot of them."

"Luke, there are more town folk than them."

"But they won't fight," Luke said. "Hell, they are just regular folks. Even we are. You and Dan are the only ones besides the police that are trained for this type of violence."

"Don't underestimate what people will do to protect the ones they love. And anyway, that's why we have got to work together. Right now we may be the only chance this town has of fighting back. Now we can run off with our tail between our legs and maybe we will get to live another week, heck, we might even be able to hole up in Dan's underground bunker but eventually violence will come knocking. No matter what you have heard about violence not solving violence, at times it's the only way. Whether you like it or not, it's time to fight."

Murphy grabbed up a bag of ammo.

"This is insane. Surely we can reason with them?" Luke asked.

Murphy chuckled and pointed outside. "You think back at the library they were looking to reason with us?"

Luke looked at Edgar who shrugged.

"I'm not a violent man, Luke, but this is my home. I grew up here. My family is here."

"So… about leaving, that's a no?"

I could see the look of reservation on Luke's face. I felt the same. I wasn't ready to battle with a bunch of skinheads. We might have had anger issues and this might have been one hell of a way to unleash pent-up frustration, but killing another human? I wasn't sure I was ready for that.

"Are we going?" Edgar asked.

"Not yet. I have to contact Dan."

AMBUSH

We remained at Murphy's for another hour while he tried to make contact with Dan via a ham radio system. He sat at a desk pressing the button on the side of the mic.

"Come in Dan. This is Murphy."

All the came out of the speakers was a hum, and the odd crackle. He repeated himself over and over again. While he was doing that I went to get some food. Anything I could scrounge from the cupboards. Luke was sitting in the kitchen having a cigarette, staring at the Glock on the counter. I found a few cans of tuna, a bottle of pickled eggs and some crackers. What did this guy live on? I blew my cheeks out and closed the pantry.

"Did you know this was coming?" Luke asked in an accusing tone.

"No. I mean, they spoke about things but I assumed it was just talk."

He scoffed and blew out some smoke.

I sighed. "Look, I know you and I don't see eye to eye. But we need to put that shit aside and work together."

"Can you imagine getting dropped into enemy territory in the middle of the night? You know, skydiving in and releasing your parachute at the last minute, then wading your way through a humid jungle just to observe and report back your findings. You hear all these horror stories from veterans about getting ambushed. Tortured by the Vietcong. I'm not sure I could handle that. I think I would just shoot myself first," Luke said. He took a strong pull on his cigarette and then reached for the gun.

"Be careful with that. It's not a toy," Edgar said coming into the room.

"And how would you know, old man? You've spent your entire life under a truck. What danger is to be found there?"

"I did my time in the war."

"Oh really? You're a vet? What war?"

He never replied.

Luke scoffed. "Yeah, just as I thought. The only war you've seen, old man, is the argument between you and your old lady after she got it on with some other dude. Yeah, I heard about that. Rumor is, it was Billy's old man. I bet he gave it to her real good."

Edgar backhanded Luke across the face, then pulled him up and slammed him against the wall. "Hey, hey, Edgar, calm down." I rushed in to try and intervene but he wasn't listening.

"Yeah, old man. I was just joking."

"You ever mention my wife, I will fucking end you. You understand?"

Luke threw his hands up in the air. "Okay."

He held him tightly against the wall, Luke's feet almost dangling off the floor. He caused such a ruckus that Murphy came into the room. By then Edgar had released his grip. I backed away. For someone in his early fifties and as quiet as he was, the guy had some serious kehoners on him.

"What's going on?"

"Nothing," Edgar brushed past Murphy and he looked at me and I just grimaced. Luke was muttering something under his breath.

"Any luck?" I asked.

"No," he said.

"It's a small unit. We can take it with us, right?"

He nodded.

We began loading up the Glocks, rifles and ammo before heading out. "Take as much food as you can. Keep to canned goods. Down in that bottom cupboard in a box is beef jerky. Grab that." I looked underneath. He wasn't joking. The guy had been drying out stack loads of meat. It was encased in airtight containers. I popped them open and started filling my bag with handfuls of the sweet-smelling, chewy meat.

As we busied ourselves, Luke didn't bother helping. He was pissed off by the way that Edgar had reacted. Leaning against the wall near the window, he blew smoke rings.

"Uh, guys. Guys," Luke stammered.

"What's up?"

"I'm guessing these aren't the Avon ladies."

His nostrils flared and I knew it was trouble. I bolted over to the window and peeked out. Coming up the driveway were four skinheads.

"Murphy."

He was out in the hallway zipping up one of the bags. He got up and grabbed his Glock, he loaded a magazine and put the gun behind his back. A few seconds later we heard the sound of boots coming up onto his porch. Murphy didn't wait, he unlocked the door but kept the chain on it.

"Can I help you guys?"

"Possibly." One of them went to push his way in but Murphy pressed back against the door.

"Look, we don't want trouble."

"Open the fucking door now or I will blow a fucking hole in your head."

"You don't want to do this. Walk away."

Murphy gave them a chance. I heard them scoff then

the one guy began kicking at the door.

What happened next occurred so quick, I just stood there with my jaw hanging down.

Murphy undid the lock and as he opened the door in one smooth motion he pulled the Glock from behind his back. Four bullets later and they were dead. The first three went down fast but the other tried to run. He'd made it halfway down the driveway before he collapsed. All of them were shot in the head.

"Come on, help me get 'em around back."

Killing was as easy to him as breathing.

Luke and I stood there staring while Murphy and Edgar went out.

"Are you going to help?" he called out. I hurried out and looked down at one of the bodies. A dark hole in his head seeped out thick blood. I didn't recognize them. My eyes darted to the driveway to check if there were any more. If they had made it this far west in the town, for all we knew there could have been another fifty down the road. Had they heard the gunfire? I took the dead guy's wrists and Luke grabbed a handful of jean around his ankles and we hauled him around the rear of the house. Murphy had a shed with a metal door on the front. He unhinged the lock and swung it wide. Inside was an old lawn mower and a few garden tools. Murphy dumped the guy he was holding, went inside the shed and grabbed up two large cans of gasoline. He brought them out and set them down nearby. He then proceeded to drag the next guy into the shed. He fished through the skinhead's jacket and pulled out a knife. He pulled a packet of cigarettes and tossed them. Luke went and collected those.

Ten minutes later they were all inside doused with gasoline.

"Luke. Lighter."

"I need it."

"I'll give it back."

Luke reluctantly handed it over. Murphy flipped it open and a flame came to life, and then he tossed it inside. A sudden burst of fire and the wooden shed was engulfed in flames. It was followed by a loud explosion.

"My lighter."

Murphy walked past him. "Time to quit."

Luke stared back at it. I think he was more surprised by the reality that he had just seen his lighter get tossed into the fire than the fact that four men had just been turned into human kebabs.

"Why would you do that?" Edgar asked.

"They might come looking for them. It's a shed, not my house."

We went back around to the front of the house, collected the bags and headed down the driveway. Edgar was about to step into the road when I pulled him back. There were others further down going house to house.

"Great, how do you suppose we get past this rabble?" Luke asked.

"You've got a weapon."

"What?"

He shoved one in Luke's hand.

"Use it."

Had it not been evening, I was certain that we would

have been spotted lingering in the shadows. We waited until the next group approached another house before making a move.

"If we get separated and you can't get back to City Hall, go to the library. Smash one of the lower windows. Chances are they won't look inside."

"No, they'll probably just set it on fire, for the heck of it," Luke said.

Crouched down behind a vehicle holding a Glock in my hand seemed surreal. Murphy indicated with two fingers when to move. None of us hesitated; we moved fast and stayed close together.

Further down the road we saw a man step out of his house with a woman and three children. One of them was a teen. They were all carrying bags, except two of the kids that were too young. They hadn't made it a few yards when five skinheads encircled them. The reactions were fast and quick, the father tried to hit one of them but he missed. The skinhead brought down a metal bar on the man's arm. He screamed. They didn't seem to care that the younger kids were under the age of ten, they just unleashed a brutal beating on them. When they stepped back, the family huddled together in the middle of the street, frightened and in tears. A skinhead with a knife moved to cut them when another stopped him.

"No, these are mine."

He brought up a metal pipe and was about to bring it down hard when a gun went off. The bullet knocked him down instantly. At first I thought it was Murphy but it wasn't. Out from one of the houses nearby came a guy with a rifle. After he had taken down the other skinhead standing near the family, he unloaded bullet after bullet as the rest of them ran at him. When the gunfire ended, he was the only one standing. The family remained frozen in place.

"Move!" Murphy shouted to them as he broke out from his position and ran towards them. The guy with the gun was an African American, he turned the gun towards Murphy.

"Whoa! I'm on your side. You need to get out of here

now, all that gunfire is going to attract them."

"I'm not going anywhere."

And with that he turned around and walked back into his house, slamming the door behind him. It was the first sign that townsfolk weren't going to just take this lying down. I raced over to where Murphy was, all the while holding my gun slightly low and looking around. Murphy told the family they either needed to get back in the house or come with us.

They stared blankly back at him. Shocked. Bruised and battered, they looked as if they were unable to process what had just happened.

"Move!" he yelled. That seemed to snap them out of their comatose state. They turned and hobbled back to their house. The father had taken the full brunt of the beating. His face was covered in blood, his clothing drenched. I caught sight of the youngest girl who had taken a hit to the ear and was bleeding. She looked at me and I know in that moment she thought I was one of them. I'd never felt so ashamed to have ever associated with the group. It wasn't about brotherhood.

These were acts of senseless violence against humans.

KILL SHOT

Society had stepped over an invisible line. I couldn't imagine every skinhead wanted to kill but people were people and they would embrace the mob mindset. When two or more were out of control it didn't take long for others to do the same. And now that the world was experiencing a blackout, the infrastructure of law and order had collapsed and the grid was down, the rules of how other humans treated others would soon go out the window, at least for the white supremacists who were assaulting anyone. They knew people wouldn't just give up generators, food or other resources. They knew that people would defend themselves. That's why they were attacking first. No questions, no requests, just brute force tactics.

It was militant in its own way. That's why we were referred to as foot soldiers. We were the ones that would go out and do the dirty work and get our hands bloody. I had never attended a skinhead rally; neither had I met those higher up in the organization, if it could even be called that. My exposure to the neo-Nazi group amounted to a small-town experience and back then law and order kept them in line. They knew their boundaries and they operated within them so as to never attract unwanted attention.

I understood that Luke and the others must have thought I had seen this coming but I hadn't. At monthly meetings, the topic of discussion centered on recruitment. Talk of how they would take back America occurred over beers. They were just words of drunken men. I had no clue that the organization was in possession of weapons of mass destruction. The very notion seemed ludicrous. How did they obtain them? I'd heard about the Cold War, spies that entered America smuggling in suitcase nukes and 84 that had gone missing. I'd read the news articles about the feds and CIA searching for them but there was no indication that the white supremacists had them. They had kept this under tight wraps. It would have been something that would have only been discussed with higher-ups. And for good reason. They didn't want to risk having anyone letting the cat out of the bag.

We retraced our steps, though this time giving a wide berth to the library. Murphy was certain that because a few survived, they would have returned to the group and no doubt that was the reason why they were banging on doors where windows were dark. Initially there wouldn't have been a need to go house to house. Supplies could be gathered from the local stores, but eventually they would have to turn their focus to homes and factories in the area.

The decision to not turn onto Pine Street but continue on Front and turn down Cedar meant we would be getting dangerously close to Main Street. It was a risk that had to be taken. The only thing we had working in our advantage was that it was a moonless night. The sky was a blanket of darkness shrouding us as we skimmed along the sides of buildings.

We had made it to the intersection of Fifth and Cedar

when Murphy stopped. We continued to move past him thinking he was just watching our back but that wasn't the case. He stepped off the curb.

"Kate?"

"Hey, hold up," I said to the others. "Murphy," I said in a half whisper.

"They've got Kate."

I ran up to join him. Peering around the corner towards Main Street which was lit up like a Mexican fiesta. A large rowdy crowd was pushing forward five police officers. One of them was Officer Kate Shaw.

"It's too late," I muttered, trying to motion for us to go.

"I'm not letting them kill her."

"There's nothing we can do, Murphy. There's too many of them. And if we continue to stand out here, we are going to be screwed ourselves."

"He's right, Murphy," Luke added.

"Go then. I'm staying. I'm not going to…" he trailed off looking at the large crowd that were riled up and preparing for a public execution. My eyes scanned the surrounding area. I was certain that at any minute another cluster of those fuckwits would show up and we'd have to engage with them. I sighed and ran a hand over my head.

"What do you want to do?"

He must have realized the predicament they were in. Had this been Iraq, no doubt more troops would have been sent in to help but there was no one else. No one was skilled to handle this kind of situation. Heck, even a riot squad would have had trouble pushing back this group. They were pumped up on liquid courage and fueling the fire in each other. With a community terrified, the police department dead or on their way to be executed, they must have seen this as a victory.

Murphy turned to say something when a loud boom rang out and he stumbled forward onto me. Behind him, further down the street, were some of the guys that we had ran into at the library. They were now charging towards us. Luke and Edgar didn't hesitate, they returned fire immediately, which slowed them up and made them dive for cover. In the dark I couldn't tell how bad Murphy had been shot, just that he got back up and told us to head east down Cedar.

Murphy slumped one arm over my shoulder and I started taking him down the street while the other two kept firing. Bullets were pinging off metal and ricocheting off concrete. A chunk of concrete hit me in the side of the face. Pain coursed through my body.

"Split up."

"Screw that."

"Just listen to me. You've got the other two-way radio. Go!"

I was still carrying a rifle in one hand and my arm was looped around his waist to support him.

"I'll take him," Edgar said rushing over. They darted across the road while Luke and I provided cover. I raced down an alley, and Luke did the same. Within a matter of minutes we were off the main stretch. In between the buildings it was even darker. My eyes scanned for anywhere I could hide. Upon reaching a chain-link fence, I slid the gun case beneath it then scrambled over. With a Glock in my hand, my heart was pounding against my chest. All I could think about was getting caught and having my face smashed in with a hammer. Fear permeated and caused sweat to drench my shirt. As I dropped to the other side I heard a couple of skinheads coming down the alley. Their boots pounded against the asphalt. Had they seen me? I hurried across the gravel and ducked behind a large green dumpster. The stench coming from it was putrid but that was the least of my concerns. My pulse sent blood rushing to my head and I felt a wave of dizziness. I pressed my back firmly against the dumpster trying to stay out of view while I cast a glance to my left and right. The only thing between them and me was the dumpster and fence. If they decided to jump over, I was going to be in a fight for my life.

I willed my breath to slow. The thought of them hearing the radio made me tremble.

They rushed by and I breathed out a sigh of relief. I

pulled the backpack off my shoulder and fished around for the radio. I waited for a minute or two before I tried to contact them.

"Guys? Come in," I muttered in a hushed voice. There was no answer. All the while my eyes were focused ahead. It was the first time I was actually grateful for the blackout. If the power weren't out, this place would have been lit up like a Christmas tree with security lights. As it was, it was like being inside a dark room with a few pinpricks of light from the night sky.

"Murphy?"

I turned up the volume ever so slightly, then wondered if they were in the same predicament as me. Was I giving away their location? I was listening so intently for a reply from them that when the sound of boots hit the dumpster behind me a cold shaft of fear shot through me. Laughter broke out as I looked up. Above me, standing on the dumpster looking down was a skinhead.

"Boo!" he said then broke into laughter. As I scrambled to my feet with the Glock in my hand and began backing away I didn't see the other one come up behind me. He rushed and hit me so hard in the center of the back I didn't know if it was his knee or boot. I slammed against the ground and the Glock flew out of my hand and slid a few feet away.

I scrambled for it but one of them stood on my fingers.

"It's the turncoat."

The guy crouched down in front of me, then looked at his buddy. "I hate a lot of things," he then began reeling off his racist remarks. "But there is nothing more that grinds my hump than a turncoat. What about you, Steve?"

"Fucking hate 'em."

With that said he yanked me up and slammed me against the dumpster and began laying into me, while the other one laughed. All my attempts at shielding the beating only riled him up even more.

"Get your fucking hands out of the way."

I attempted to fight back but his buddy stepped in to

take over. A second later I was spitting blood on the asphalt. Breathing hard and looking ahead I didn't see the kick come in from the side. There was no time to brace for it. I sucked in air and then felt the sole of his boot come down twice on my back as if he was trying to crush my spine. As I was slumped there, one of them went over and picked up the Glock.

"Nice piece, I think I'll take that." He tucked it into his waistband. I pushed myself up and leaned back against the dumpster. "They are going to fucking love you when we take you back."

Call it pent-up rage or just an adrenaline rush but as he came back to give me another pounding, I reacted.

He grabbed the back of my collar and I came up with a swift uppercut that took him off balance. I charged him and grabbed the handle of the Glock from the front of his pants but instead of yanking it out I pulled the trigger. The bullet shot through his leg as I collapsed on top of him. His scream was deafening. In that split second I was in survival mode. There was no time to pull the gun out as the other guy came at me. Before he got within two feet, another gunshot went off and the guy dropped. Still on the skinhead who was squirming beneath me in agony, I saw Luke out the corner of my eye. He'd hopped over the fence. I stumbled back to catch my breath when the second round was fired. Luke loomed over him with the gun still pointed at his head. He had killed both of them. I could see that his hand was shaking.

"You okay?"

I spit blood on the floor, then nodded. "Not exactly."

Everything seemed surreal in that moment. I don't know what I expected to see in his face. Remorse perhaps? Guilt? God, he'd just killed two people.

He motioned with his head. "Go up. Murphy and Edgar are on the roof across from here. You still got the radio?"

"Yeah," I replied. With that he turned and dashed off into the darkness leaving me beside two dead bodies. I stared at one. He couldn't have been more than nineteen years of age. I felt my stomach churn within me and I flipped over and vomited. I wiped my lips with the back of my arm and then staggered to my feet. I removed the gun from the dead guy's waistband, moved quickly over to the rifle case and grabbed it up. I headed in the direction of where Luke had gone. He whistled from a building one block down, then pointed to a black fire escape that went up the side of a four-story building. I juggled the rifle case in one hand and began making my way up. Once I heaved it over the top, I slumped down and took a moment to get my bearings. All over the city the sound of gunshots resounded. The community was fighting back. Maybe we weren't alone. Whether we would win was to be seen.

"Sam, you there?"

Murphy's voice came from the two-way. I pressed the button, cleared my throat. "Go ahead."

"You okay?"

What was it with everyone asking me that? No, I fucking wasn't okay. I had been shot at, slapped around and had witnessed people murdered in front of me. I was far from okay.

"How's the bleeding?" I asked.

"It's under control."

I had images of him stuffing dirt into the hole or a piece of cloth. These military guys were badass and they knew all manner of ways to stop bleeding. Gunfire echoed in the darkness.

"Do you have a bead on Kate?"

"A bead?"

He replied sounding frustrated. "Can you see her?"

I got up and went over to the edge, while trying to remain low. I was at the top of a building that was on the corner of Cedar and Fourth. I could see Main Street and the angry mob. Cars were on fire; black smoke swirled up and vanished in the blackness of night.

"Take out the rifle, use the scope."

I went back to the case and lugged it over. I unclipped the side and flipped it open. It smelled like fresh leather. The rifle had some weight to it when I took it out.

"Do you have it?"

I pressed the button. "I got it."

"Tell me what you see."

I rested the rifle on the edge of the building and peered through the scope. I adjusted it slightly and then tilted it down. Lots of heads, fists, and angry faces. I swept back and forth until I came to rest on the officers who were on their knees.

"I see her."

"Keep your eyes on the guy walking back and forth in front of them."

I couldn't hear what was being said.

Drifting up was just pure noise, music blaring and skinheads cheering and pumping the air with fists. Several of them were firing off rounds as if already celebrating.

"My arm is fucked so I'm going to need you to take the shot."

"What?"

"You are going to have to take the shot otherwise she is going to die."

I peered again through the scope and spotted a

handgun in the hand of the man who was walking up and down.

"Why not Edgar or Luke?"

"There's not time for questions. The other two are positioned on different roofs. When you fire, they will fire too, they aren't going to know who took the shot. That should give you enough time to get down. After you get back to City Hall, distribute the weapons. We are going to need the additional help."

In my backpack were several handguns. Inside the case was a rifle and a Benelli M4 Tactical shotgun.

"Why don't you…"

"My arm is shot, Sam. You're the one carrying the rifle. I've got my M4 Carbine. That will keep them at bay for a while."

"And the others?"

"They have AR-15's, they should be okay."

None of this was sinking in. It was like being thrown in at the deep end. There was no easing into any of this.

"I don't think I can do this."

Murphy interjected. "Sam, this is not the time to back away."

"But—"

"You are in a war, whether you like it or not. They won't hesitate to kill. It's simple, do you want those officers dead?"

I hesitated before I replied. "No."

"Then you need to pull the trigger."

"I've only ever fired a rifle when I've gone hunting."

"Then you should be fine," Luke muttered over the radio.

There was a pause in our conversation; I assumed Murphy was reassessing the situation from his position.

"Luke, once he takes the shot and you fire some rounds, I want you to change position. We need to keep moving. Give them the sense that there are more of us than there really are. And Sam, I hope you can run fast."

I didn't reply.

"Sam, did you hear me?"

I pressed down on the button. "Yep."

As I peered through the scope, Murphy told me to take the shot. I checked that there was a round in the chamber. I focused in on the guy who was now standing in front of one of the male officers. He lifted his gun and fired a round into his head. The sound of Kate's scream could be heard. The armed skinhead then stepped to his left to repeat the process.

"Sam. Take the shot!"

I froze in that moment. It was long enough for the man to shoot another cop. There were three remaining. Kate was in the middle.

"Take the shot!"

I exhaled hard. My finger squeezed against the trigger and the bullet hit its target.

The skinhead fell on the officer and before the others could figure out where the shot came from, Murphy, Edgar and Luke began unloading rounds into the large group.

It was pure pandemonium.

People were climbing on top of each other to get out

from the rain of bullets that were taking down the group from multiple angles, and different locations.

I pulled the rifle back into the case, closed it and got the hell off that roof.

FINE LINE

I couldn't believe I had just killed someone. I didn't even have time to process it. I was down on the ground and pounding the pavement back to Cedar Street. The streets would be crawling with them as some sought cover, while others looked to find the shooters. On one hand I didn't want to leave them but I was following orders, running on instinct and had smothered the emotion that was in danger of paralyzing me. A mix of fear and adrenaline kept my legs moving. My thighs screamed in protest, and I could feel a stitch coming on.

I saw the sign for Seventh Street up ahead. It was one block over. I still had to cross Sixth Street. As I burst across the street a batch of skinheads plowed into me. One of them fell to the ground. A few of them I recognized. My eyes scanned their faces hoping to god that they weren't any of the guys from the library.

"Frost, where the hell have you been?"

It was Bryan Catz. He grabbed a hold of me.

"We were getting fired at, I ran just like you."

"Did you see where it came from?"

"Back there."

I motioned over my shoulder and he glanced down at the case in my hand and frowned. "What the fuck is that?"

I swallowed hard as he pulled it out of my hand. Other skinheads ran past us, only Bryan and a couple others had stopped. They were looking around nervously. Fear on their faces. The idea of standing out in the open was probably making them antsy. He pushed me back and placed the case on the ground. I reached around my back and took a hold of the Glock. I began taking several steps back towards Seventh Street as he unlocked the case. I didn't stick around to see his reaction. I turned and ran. I glanced back when I heard him call my name.

"Frost! You fucker. Get him."

And that was it. If I had a stitch before, my stomach felt like it was about to hurl as I raced towards Seventh

Street with multiple skinheads on my tail. I turned a few times to fire a couple of rounds to slow them down but that only infuriated them more. As I zigzagged to avoid being hit by a bullet, I fixed my face like a flint towards Seventh Street. When I reached it, I could see City Hall one block down.

The only thing pushing through my mind was to get to that building.

At the far end of the road I saw more skinheads running up towards me. They were probably the overflow from Main Street. While they weren't aware of the others chasing me, I wasn't going to risk it. I dashed into an alley, pushed the Glock into the back of my waistband and sprinted hard down the dirt-filled street full of puddles left over from rain. Water splashed up my leg and my throat felt like it was on fire as I turned back to see Bryan and six others racing after me.

I was fucked. Royally.

I turned a corner and practically launched myself up onto a dumpster and over the fence. As I landed hard the

Glock fell out of my waistband. I had only taken a few steps when I heard it hit the ground. I swiveled back and scooped it up just as one of them came over the fence. He was in midair about to land when I fired into him, then fired two more rounds at the fence. That kept the others back but not for long. As I got closer to the rear doors of City Hall, I knew that there was a shitload of chairs and tables stacked up behind them. There was no way that I was going to be able to get inside, and if any of the five skinheads behind me realized that others were there, they would swarm the place.

Shit! I screamed inwardly as I changed direction and flew into a tight alley that had overgrown with weeds, branches and brambles. Nature tore at my skin like gnarled fingers. I felt as though I was running into a black hole.

As I came out the other side, I sprinted across the street and into a large patch of trees between a maintenance and building supplies store and an auto dealership. I ran up to the first door and yanked on it hard but it was locked. Before I could get to the wall that hedged in the two buildings, I heard them.

I ducked down behind a huge supply of lumber.

"Frost, I know you are in here."

I heard their boots nearby, one of them smashed a window on a car with his baseball bat. It happened again, then again.

"Come on out. I'll give you a chance to explain yourself to Eli. Perhaps he'll show mercy on you and just take away your red shoelaces." Eli? I heard a couple of them laugh. They were playing games with me. There was no way out. It was made very clear at the beginning. If you went against them, you got fucked up. And with the way things were now, fucked up meant dead.

I shifted my position as I saw one of them getting closer. I moved over to a red SUV and got between two of them. I laid on the ground. From there I could see their boots. I pulled out the magazine and checked how many rounds I had left, and then slid it back in. I had more than enough to kill all five of them but they were also packing. At least one of them was. The others had baseball bats, a chain and something else that would no doubt tear me apart.

"You know Nate was a good guy, he was like a brother to me."

He must have been referring to the guy I'd shot near City Hall. That was two people I had killed. Though the second time around, it was different. I knew it was him or me. I wiped moisture from my lips and looked to my right. In the window of one of the cars I saw the reflection of a flashlight. I moved position for a second time. I wasn't going to be able to hide for long. On the other hand I didn't want to kill any more people.

We were going to need the bullets. I moved into the section of used vehicles and began checking the trunks on each of them while keeping low to the ground. Several times they passed by the vehicle I was behind. All that could be heard was gravel beneath their boots and the occasional whack as they slammed a baseball bat against metal.

At what point does a man break when pushed into a corner? What happens when the lines blur between what he doesn't want to do and that which he must? Murphy's words came back to me. They were words he'd shared when we were out in the wilderness. The second month was meant to be harder. That it was. Every day out there in the elements he imparted lessons to us. Some of them just went in one ear and out the other but others stuck.

Murphy had been reeling off one of his old war stories about him and his buddies caught in a firefight. According to him, his platoon had been sent in to rescue a group of U.S. military advisers when they got overrun. A massive coalition air strike was called in. They destroyed over forty buildings and killed over seventy militants but it wasn't enough.

There is a fine line that separates those that will and those that won't. There is a fine line between those that will stand and those that will fall. While you are out here that line for you might be as simple as hiking another mile. On the frontline, where lives are lost or survive, it means pulling the trigger when you might just want to freeze or run. I don't like killing people but if it means bringing the guy beside me home alive, I won't hesitate. Now dig deep, dig d-e-e-p.

His words echoed in my mind as I became one hundred percent focused on getting out of this alive. I crept up the back of the van I had moved behind and peered through the murky glass. I could see two of them at one o'clock, one was at twelve and the others were at nine. Like sheep that had strayed from the pack. I focused on the one at twelve. I crouched down and positioned myself at the corner of the van with the Glock extended.

I was waiting for the moment he came into view. I swallowed hard, every ounce of my being was focused on the tunnel, the gap between the vehicles. As he walked into frame, I aimed and pulled the trigger. The moment he went down, I rolled out into a new position further down and further back.

"Where did that come from?"

One down.

I moved again. This time I was nervous to look around the corner of the next vehicle in the event that they spotted me. The two guys who were at one o'clock had raced over to check on their buddy who was now lying motionless. I circled around another vehicle. As I stuck my head out to take a look, one of them spotted me and pointed.

"There he is."

A spray of bullets from whoever was carrying hit the car. A window shattered and I heard Bryan telling them to split up. My pulse had gone into overdrive. Everything became crystal-clear as though I had too much caffeine. Fear no longer crippled me, all I had left now was my fight-or-flight instinct and flight was off the radar.

I stared into a window and saw the reflection of one of them creeping up the side with a large knife in his hand. The ground beneath me was nothing more than gravel. I took a handful of it and tossed it towards the tree line. When I saw him turn, I came out and fired a round into him then ducked back out of sight.

I could hear them cursing.

"Give me that," I heard Bryan scream.

"Come on."

He fired off four rounds in frustration in multiple directions.

"This is not over, Frost."

I then heard their feet pound the ground and become distant. As I looked over they were gone. Two down and the other three had run.

I breathed out hard, went over to the guy who was closest to me and checked his pockets. I grabbed a packet of cigarettes out, banged one out and lit it. I coughed hard. *Shit, I need to give these up.* I peered over the hood of a car, took the knife from the guy and pinched the bridge of my nose. I felt something sticky and wiped my mouth with my hand. As I looked at it, I saw it was covered in blood. But it wasn't mine. It was his.

The smell of iron, and its taste on my lips made my stomach turn again. I brought a hand up to my mouth to stop myself from throwing up for the second time that evening.

RISKY BUSINESS

I returned to City Hall by cutting through the maintenance supply building and a health food store. When they opened the back door, Billy rushed me inside and cast a nervous glance around. Ally took one look at me and then craned her head to see if her father was behind.

"Where is he?"

I was panting and out of breath. I placed a hand on my knee and pulled the backpack off my shoulder. "He's been shot."

"What?" she screamed.

"He's alive but he needs our help."

I passed the two-way to them and they tried getting through to Murphy but there was no answer. That only increased their anxiety. I couldn't imagine he would answer. By now the skinheads would be crawling all over the place trying to get at them. I just hoped they were still alive.

I unzipped the bag and turned it over. The contents went all over the floor. There were four handguns of various makes, Glock, Browning, Ruger and Sig Sauer. In addition to this were several boxes of ammo.

Both Sara and Ally kept peppering me with questions but I couldn't answer them. First because they were asking at the same time, and second because I had this ringing in my ears from shooting the last guy.

"Give the kid some space," Matt said getting between them and me. "Just give him a minute to catch his breath."

An older woman came up with a bottle of water. I thanked her and chugged it down then took a seat. Billy grabbed up one of the handguns and began loading it.

"Do you know what you're doing with that, boy?" an older man with grey hair said.

"I'm not a boy, old man." He popped out the magazine and began loading bullets one on top of the next. Once he had it filled he slapped it in the bottom and loaded one in the chamber.

I brought them up to speed on what had taken place with Kate. I saw the look in Sara's eyes. There was obviously something going on there. Perhaps Murphy was seeing her on the side. Maybe that was what had caused their marriage to fall apart.

"Anyone who wants to stay, stay. I'm going with him," Matt said taking one of the guns and loading it. Sara frowned and grabbed his arm. She shook her head.

"I'm not losing you."

"He needs our help."

Ally grabbed one of the guns.

"Oh no you don't," Sara said taking the weapon from her hand.

"If dad is in trouble, I'm going."

"No, she's right, you need to stay here," Matt said.

"I'll go," Corey added.

Raymond Wells, an insurance agent, pushed his way forward. "Don't be a fool, boy. You are just a kid." He tried to take the gun from Corey, but that was the worst thing he could do.

Corey pushed him back. "Get the fuck off me."

"You need someone to teach you manners," he shot back.

"What? And you're the guy to do it?"

Raymond moved forward. "Just like your father, he was a loser."

Corey lifted the gun at him, holding it in some kind of gangster angle, like he'd seen on TV. "You better back up, bitch."

Billy started laughing.

"Shut the fuck up."

"Oh what, you going to make me?" Billy raised his weapon. A few gasps came from the oldies and Matt tried to intervene. Things were spiraling out of control real fast.

"Guys, this isn't helping Murphy," I said.

There was a moment of awkward tension and then Billy lowered his weapon. If only Murphy could have seen this. We really needed six months with him. He had only begun to scratch the surface of our problems. The friction between Billy and Corey had been ongoing since day one of our arrival at Camp Zero. Billy had been acting like he was mentally insane in an attempt to get himself sent home and Corey was the first one to see through his charade. From then on out, they had been at each other's throats.

"I'm just saying, you're not old enough to fire a handgun," Raymond said.

"Are you willing to go out there? Do you want to face those skinheads?" Corey asked.

Raymond's chin dropped a little.

"That's what I thought."

"Corey, he has a point," Sara tried to provide a voice of reason.

"Well then, let's put it to a vote. If there are four adults who want to go, fine. We'll stay."

Corey looked over to Billy.

"Speak for yourself. I'm going," Billy replied.

"Three then."

Another icy glare was exchanged; thankfully handguns

weren't waved around this time. Matt asked people to raise their hands if they wanted to help. We could tell within the first thirty seconds that no one wanted to go out there. It was risky business and the chances of coming back were slim.

"Then it's settled," Corey said picking his gun back up and moving out with a box of ammo in the other hand. I don't think it was as much a matter of bravery as it was that he really didn't give two shits about his life.

"I'll go," Brett said.

"That's five."

Corey, Billy, Matt, Brett and me.

"No, Brett, they will lynch you," Jodi said.

"Then so be it. I'm not going to sit by watching them destroy our town."

"Maybe you don't need to."

I was eyeing Ally from across the room. "Did your old man ever teach you how to fire a gun?"

She let out a chuckle. "I could shoot a cap off a bottle from fifty yards."

"Yeah, right," Billy said before mimicking puppet movements with his hand as though she was all talk.

"Let's put a cap on your head then."

"Screw you."

"Hey," Matt said coming to her defense.

"She's not going out, Sam," Sara said. "Trained or not, I won't risk it."

"Fair enough."

It was interesting to see the level of concern that she had for her. Brett and Jodi? They were different. They had what I classed as a vested interest in me. I just wasn't sure what it was.

"Let's go," Matt said.

A few hugs were exchanged while Corey and Billy pulled back the chairs and tables from behind the door. I glanced at the clock. It was a little after eleven at night. Billy shouldered the door and surveyed the area outside. It was so damn dark that if any skinheads were waiting to pop us the moment we came out, we would have died for sure. Thankfully, as far as I knew, no one was aware that anyone was inside City Hall. It would have been one of the last places to check. They would have gone to homes and raided businesses long before they approached any government building. Then of course there was the police station that was directly beside it.

Getting back wasn't an easy task. The streets were filled with them. It was like a war zone. The sound of gunfire could still be heard.

"You think they're still alive?"

"As long as they haven't run out of ammo and are on top of the roofs. There is only one way up onto those roofs."

"I don't like this one bit," Matt said.

We stayed in a line with Corey and Brett keeping an eye on the rear, while Billy and I forged ahead. It took us the better part of fifteen minutes to get close to the block where Luke had killed the two guys.

"Just follow the sound of rapid gunfire. That has to be Murphy."

We were down between two buildings in a narrow

dark alley when the first wave of attacks began. They must have seen us coming as it happened so fast. I don't even know where they were hiding as it was so damn dark. One of us managed to get a round off but after that it was all hands on. One of the skinheads wielded his bat, I ducked and shouldered his gut taking him to the floor. Jab after jab, I unleashed a flurry of hits on him until someone kicked me in the face.

The sound of another gun went off and then they stopped.

"Don't you fucking move!"

Matt was holding his gun out and waving it around and for a few brief seconds I thought we were in the clear. When the baseball bat came swinging out of the darkness and hit him square in the face, I think we all winced. The gun went off and the brawling began again. I scrambled to my feet and threw as many punches as I could get in. It was hard to see who was winning as it was like a mosh pit in the dark. Arm, legs, hands, groans of pain and then I was being pulled off the guy whose face I had pummeled.

"Sam."

I swung around instinctively and nearly took out Brett.

"That's enough."

I looked down at the guy whose face was bloodied and beaten to a pulp. My hands were shaking. I stared at the back of my raw knuckles. The shock didn't set in until I saw Matt further down from us. He lay motionless.

"Matt?"

"He's dead. We need to go," Brett said pushing on.

All of us looked as if we had been dragged through a bush backwards. Bruised, battered but still alive we pressed on until we reached the building I'd been on. I tried communicating with Murphy but there was still no answer. We climbed up and that's when we got a better view of what was going on. Skinheads were on the tops of various buildings and were firing at one that held all three of them. Luke, Murphy and Edgar were returning fire. Crouched down low we assessed the situation. I tried to communicate again but they weren't picking up. The noise of gunfire was deafening. It was like the Battle of

Mogadishu, except none of us were soldiers and none of us had training on what to do. We were fortunate to have survived so far through brute force of will. Matt hadn't been so lucky. It could have been any one of us.

"We aren't going to be able to help them from here. These handguns won't give us the distance."

I peered over the edge into the streets to see where the officers were. The crowd had dispersed. The only light came from cars that were on fire. I could see bodies everywhere. There had to have been at least sixty or seventy people dead.

I pulled back and slumped down behind the brick wall. The others were watching the mayhem when the radio crackled. "Sam."

It was Luke.

"Yeah."

"You got the others?"

"Three."

"Three!" he stammered and I pulled the speaker away from my ear.

"That's it," I replied.

"Murphy wants you to go find Shaw."

"Oh, I'll just stroll on into the chaos down below and locate her. Are you out of your mind?"

"That's his words not mine. Hold up."

The sound of gunfire intensified for a minute or two. I peered over the edge and could see that some skinheads had attempted to go up the side of the building. One was carrying a lit Molotov cocktail. Luke shot the guy before he had a chance to toss it. Instead it dropped and smashed over the two below him. They fell off the side of the building covered in flames, screaming.

"Sorry about that. Some asshole was at the door," Luke continued.

"Tell Murphy we've lost the rifle and shotgun. But we still have the handguns."

"Any other good news?" Luke enquired.

I hesitated before speaking into the mic. "Matt's dead."

There was silence on the other end. I was expecting

Billy to make a crack about how having his ex's boyfriend out of the picture might have been good news. But he didn't.

"I got to go."

I waited there for a few seconds looking over the tops of the roofs.

"Well, you heard him."

"He expects us to go back down there?" Billy asked.

"Kate could die."

"So could hundreds of other people. Why should she be treated any different?" Billy asked. "Hell, my family is out there too. He wants us to risk our neck for some cop? The same one that busted our ass multiple times?" He paused. "No, screw that. If he has a death wish he can go down there and save her. I came here to help these guys get back to City Hall."

"And then what?"

"We hunker down until the cavalry shows up."

"The military have their hands full, Billy. No one is coming."

"There are thousands of military personnel on aircraft carriers. The military is coming."

"Even if they make it back to land, you think they are going to come to our little neck of the woods? They are going to focus on continuity of government and the largest cities first."

"I don't give a shit what you think."

"And what? You think these skinheads are going to sit by and wait? We have just opened up a can of worms, kicked a hornet's nest and unleashed hell on this town."

"That wasn't my call."

"No, no it wasn't but you're in it now. If you didn't want to help then you shouldn't have come."

"Oh screw you, Sam."

"Guys," Brett said, gesturing with his head out across the town. We followed his gaze to a group that was coming up the street carrying Molotov cocktails.

"Oh shit."

I got up and ran over to the edge and began making my way down. Corey and Brett followed suit. Billy was the only one that hesitated and the only reason I think he moved was because he didn't want to be left alone. As soon as my boots hit the floor I broke into a fast-paced jog keeping my gun low and hugging the sides of the buildings. Once I made it to the corner of the U.S. Post Office, I crouched down in a comfortable position. Corey took up a spot behind a burnt-out car. Brett climbed up a small pipe that led to an overhang on a building and laid down. Billy came up behind me and was droning on about how we were all going to end up dead.

"Good, maybe then I will get some peace from listening to you."

He huffed and took a spot over by Corey. We watched the group get closer to the side of the building.

"Wait."

They stopped and looked around for a few seconds before beginning to climb. I no longer thought about not wanting to kill. The thought didn't even cross my mind. We had no other option. We weren't going to let Murphy and the others die up there. They were already under heavy gunfire from across the roofs. It was a means to distract them while another group attempted to come up the other fire escape. Even if Luke could hold them off, it was only a matter of time before they ran out of ammo.

I focused on the one beginning to climb, aiming for his back. A short pause. A final second and then I fired. The moment I did so, the others did also. The guy fell causing the Molotov cocktail to set alight the ground around their feet. Chaos erupted as others began returning fire at our unexpected attack. The only advantage we had was there were no vehicles nearby us that were on fire, so we were shrouded by the darkness of night. However that didn't stop them from firing wildly at us. When Luke leaned over and started raining bullets down on them, they retreated back like rats into the sewers.

"Move out," Corey said.

Stepping out from behind the vehicle he rushed across the road and took cover while continuing to fire. We covered each other as we tried to close the gap between us and the building. I radioed up.

"Get ready to go," I shouted.

Murphy got on the line this time. "No, we're aren't going yet. We need to get Shaw and the other cops."

"I admire your heart, Murphy, you get ten for effort but Shaw could be anywhere by now."

"She's not. They dragged them inside the church."

"Yeah, and probably executed them."

"I have to know."

"And you expect us to go in there with nothing more than handguns?"

"I don't expect you to do anything. If you want to run, hide or get out of town, that's your choice. But I'm not leaving without her."

"Matt is dead," I said.

He didn't even pause. "He knew the risk coming out."

And that was it, nothing more than a passing comment before he was back to yelling out orders to Luke.

"Are you with us?" he asked.

"You want to define that?" I said while firing off two more rounds at a skinhead who was trying to make his way up to us with an AK47 in his hand. A flurry of bullets came from him, which forced us down on the ground.

I heard Billy screaming something. I turned and saw that he had pissed himself out of fear. I didn't imagine that was the worst of what was seen by military when they were under attack. I was expecting at least one of us to curl into a ball and cry. This wasn't a game. Those were real rounds flying at us and we all knew we could die.

SHAW

War. I had never been in one but the thought had crossed my mind of signing up for the military. There was something very admirable about those who defended the country. It wasn't like they got paid a lot. A recruiter had once visited our school and that was one of the questions that somebody asked. It was then followed by another about why would anyone do it if it paid badly? The recruiter just smiled and shook his head. It was as if words could never clearly convey why. Sure, some joined because they had no other goals but that didn't account for all those eager to get out there on the frontlines. What drove them? What pushed them to want to risk their life? I had heard of soldiers willing to die rather than leave behind one of their own but never understood it. There had to have been some kind of bond forged by battle itself.

More bullets were shot overhead by the lunatic with

the AK47. I'll never forget the look on his face. He truly believed that what he was fighting for was right even if innocent people died in the process. But then again, wasn't all war like that? Both sides believing that they were defending their own families, beliefs and way of life?

"We are pinned down," I yelled into the hand-held radio. The bullets continued for several more minutes before they stopped. When I raised my head the guy was on the floor. I glanced up at the roof to see that Murphy had taken him out.

"Go get his weapon."

What headspace did this guy have to operate in to act the way he did? He must have thought we were fearless. In all honesty I was overcome by fear but it was like being thrown in an icy lake. The initial shock was always the worst. The body and mind soon adjusted to the situation. I rushed forward on all fours trying to keep below the hail of bullets. One of the other skinheads must have had the same idea as I saw him bolting towards the weapon at the same time. He cast me a glance and unloaded several rounds. Fortunately the guy had the accuracy of a blind man. One of my bullets struck him in the side and he collapsed in agony. When I pried loose the AK47 from the dead man's hands, I turned in time to feel the brunt force of a boot in the side of my head. I was knocked back and startled as a skinhead landed on top of me and began trying to choke me using the very weapon I had tried to get. The hate in his eyes as he pressed down on the gun was palpable. When a round struck him in the side of the head, he became a dead weight on top of me. I glanced to my side to see Corey.

With blood sprayed on my face, I heaved him off and then fished around inside the pockets of the dead guy who originally had the gun. I pulled out a box of bullets, and another magazine. Snagging them and seeking shelter behind a car I radioed over to Murphy who was our eyes in the sky.

"How many are there?"

"Do you really want me to answer that?" he shot back.

"Maybe not." I snorted as I jammed the next magazine

into the AK47. Tucking my Glock behind my back I slung the gun up into position and readied myself. Brett came down from the side of the building while Corey and I took the left side of the street. The back windshield on a car nearby shattered and I returned a flurry of bullets.

The church was approximately two blocks from us. We would fire then hustle ass behind the next car using them as shields against the torrent of fire. We had to have eyes in the back of our heads as those bastards were everywhere and not all of them were wielding bats, chains and machetes. Corey kept his eyes behind me while I focused ahead. We had to hope that Murphy and the others were at least covering those we couldn't see.

I'm not sure how long we were on that street but it felt like hours and every second of it was as terrifying as the next. What we hadn't seen was that Murphy and the others had decided to make their way down, and were coming up the rear.

When we reached the church, I wanted to go around the back and see if we could find a way inside but when

Murphy caught up to us. He said he was going to create a distraction at the front, Billy, Corey and I would take the back. We moved fast. All the while trying to not get shot in the process. At the rear of the church was a large green dumpster and a pair of double doors. Billy tugged on them and they opened.

"Murphy, we're in."

We heard gunfire from the front and we assumed that was our cue to move. Billy pulled the door and I stood off to one side. Satisfied that no one was in the back, we slipped in. It was dark inside; there wasn't even a smidgen of light for a short while. Quietly we shuffled through the corridor and passed several offices that were empty. At the end of the hall, there was another large door. I slung the AK47 under my arm. It hung from the strap loosely behind me as I cracked the door open ever so slowly. Inside the sanctuary it was lit up with candles that flickered and cast shadows on the walls.

Near the rear of the sanctuary a skinhead had an AK47 aimed at the three cops. One of which was Kate Shaw. At the front, were three more.

I pulled back closing the door so it didn't make a noise. With two fingers I motioned for them to go down to one of the offices. When we got there I told them how many there were inside.

"If we just unload on them, there is a chance the cops will get caught up in the crossfire."

"Isn't there usually a door on either side?"

"We are going to have to clear it fast. I'll take out the guy watching over them, while you two focus on the three up front," I said.

"Got it."

"Billy, you go to the other side. We'll enter through here. The moment I fire that round, you are going to have to shift ass."

He nodded. I could tell all of us were as nervous as hell. There were three lives hanging in the balance, six if we included ourselves. We moved into position and waited for Billy to crack the door on the other side. Instead of waiting for us he burst through the door and started firing at the three at the front. If I didn't have the barrel of my gun already aimed at the guy at the rear, Billy would have been dead. The clatter of gunfire echoed loudly around the high ceilings. I wished it could have been over quickly, but it wasn't. Two of the guys near the front had managed to duck down and they were now returning fire on us. I scrambled across the floor to the police officers who were face down. Sharp slivers of wood shot all over the place as bullets tore through pews destroying what must have cost thousands of dollars.

"Sam?" Kate looked on astonished.

"Oh hey, just thought I would drop in to light a candle."

I reached over and untied her hands from behind her back and handed her the Glock. By the time she was up it was over. Murphy had come through the front and taken out the other two.

Silence filled the church if only for a few minutes. I cast a glance up at Christ on a cross. I wasn't religious but I sure as hell was ready to believe in a higher power if it meant getting out of this alive.

Officer Shaw rushed up to Murphy and right then I could tell their relationship wasn't strictly business. He pulled her tight and kissed her. The other two officers motioned to be let out of their binds.

"Right, hold on," I said beginning to loosen their ties.

"You fucking idiot," were the first words I heard. They came from the mouth of Corey.

"Oh crap." Corey was about to go nuclear on Billy for opening fire before we had got in.

"So what, I shot first. You're alive."

"Barely."

"Get over it," Billy replied.

"I swear I will put a bullet in you, if you do that again."

Billy scoffed and backed away.

"We should go," Murphy said. The others nodded and we exited out the back. As we came out and circled the building, we were about to cross over the parking lot and head towards City Hall when we heard someone's voice bellowing over a megaphone. Immediately we looked around at our group.

"Where's Edgar?" Murphy asked.

The voice coming from the megaphone was Edgar's. The next voice was deeper and huskier.

"Lay down your weapons."

"Where's that coming from?" Corey said. Down the alley that went along the side of the church a large group skinheads came into view. We pulled back to get out of the direct line of sight.

"We have your friend. Now unless you want to see his blood spilled, I suggest you do as I say. Lay down your weapons."

The officers shook their heads. I looked to Murphy, he squeezed his eyes closed. I could see he was still in pain from the gunshot wound.

"Who are you?" Murphy shouted out.

"My name is Eli Pope, I am one of the leaders of the Aryan Brotherhood. And you are?"

We kept our eyes peeled for anyone who might come

up from behind us. Billy and Corey went to the corners.

"Come on, I've told you my name. Now I'd like to know who has been killing my men."

"It doesn't matter," Murphy shouted out.

"Oh it matters," the man replied through his echoing microphone.

"You aren't going to stop, are you?"

"You can't stop change," Eli said.

"This isn't change. What you are doing is genocide."

"Genocide, cleaning the slate. It was eventually going to happen. We just sped up the process."

"What do you want?"

"This country. This town. Isn't that obvious?"

"You are killing innocent people."

There was a hesitation before Eli replied. "No one is innocent. Every single person in this country has blood on his or her hands. Whether they choose to take up a weapon or not, their actions have drawn a line in the sand. Us and them. You and I."

"Look… just let him go and we'll move out of here."

He laughed over the megaphone. "You'll move out. Move out where? We are wherever you think you are going. Do I need to explain the rest?"

"We're not laying down our weapons."

"Fair enough. Kill him."

"No!" Murphy shouted but his cry fell on deaf ears. As we stepped out, they took a machete to Edgar and sliced his throat, kicked him to the floor and then drove it down through the back of his head.

"Bastard." Murphy unleashed a flurry of rounds.

Shaw motioned for us to move. Right there in that moment the image of Edgar being murdered was burned inside my mind.

Whatever hope there was of seeing this turned around was gone.

ASSAULT

It's easy to say what a person would do in our situation but it was like being in a car wreck. This whole thing had blindsided us. War could do that to anyone. It was one thing to see it in films, read about it in books and hear from the mouths of veterans. It was another to be thrown into the fire and pitted against vile individuals.

Truth be told, I didn't think for one second that those who followed Eli Pope were one hundred percent loyal to his demented views. It was the same with any group. There would always be those that would question.

I had to wonder how many of our group had doubts about me. On the surface I was a skinhead. Sure, my hair had grown out a little but not enough to make a person not question my allegiance. I was a wild card, of that I was certain.

I couldn't believe that I had spent a year and a half with some of these people. Drank beers, partied and given my time to help them, only to witness them tear down the town around us.

Retreating from the church to City Hall wasn't an easy task. After they killed Edgar in front of us, a large group began to chase us through the streets. The noise of gunfire robbed what little peace remained.

The only way we were going to get out of this situation was together.

Fighting these people wasn't something I wanted to do. We barely had time to think clearly since this had kicked off. If this had been any other disaster, most would have focused on finding food, shelter and perhaps some protection from the fallout. Not us. It had been non-stop fighting.

How many other towns had been taken by neo-Nazi skinheads?

How many people had died while fighting to protect their loved ones?

How many were still alive in the country?

After holding off the group, those who were injured

made it back to City Hall. We joined them ten minutes later. My eyes widened as we came running and saw the doors at the rear were open. Tables and chairs were scattered outside as though the occupants inside had been in a rush to get out.

"Sara?" Murphy called out. He and the two male officers ventured inside while the rest of us kept an eye on the entrance points. Billy and Corey took a place at either corner of the building to make sure that we weren't caught by surprise.

When Murphy reappeared, he shrugged.

"They were here when we left," I said.

"Let's fan out. They couldn't have gone far. The front was smashed in. They must have come under attack or someone saw you guys come out."

It was possible. It was dark and anyone could have been lurking in the shadows. My immediate thoughts went to Bryan Catz. Had he followed me back from the auto dealership? For a brief moment I thought we might have been able to hunker down and get some relief from the fight. I was wrong. One thing for sure, the skinheads would eventually grow tired and hungry unless they were drugged up. I had seen a number of them go on three-day binges after taking meth. In those times they partied hard and looked for trouble.

"What if they tried to hike out?" I asked.

"Sara wouldn't leave. Not without Matt."

More gunfire erupted from Corey and Billy.

"Guys, whatever you are deciding to do, we should do it now," Corey yelled.

"We should get the rest of the weapons from the lockup," Shaw said.

Murphy nodded.

"We have a first-aid kit in there, we need to get that wound looked at."

Murphy shook his head. "There's no time. I need to find them."

"You aren't going to be much use to them dead. Let a few of the others go out and search while we deal with that wound."

Murphy was reluctant at first but Shaw became quite adamant that he wasn't going anywhere. It was interesting to watch him agree. Perhaps she was good for him. I'd always imagined when a person found the right woman or guy, they would be the type of person that could break through any wall of stubbornness.

As the police and fire department was attached to City Hall and Shaw had access to it, It wasn't long before we were inside. It was quiet for a short while. The walls muffled the noise of gunfire. We knew weren't the only ones fighting this battle. In some ways that was reassuring. It wasn't like the entire town would have rolled over and let them take whatever they wanted. There were some nutcases in our town, and those who were ex-military. They were the kind of folks that would have put up a fight, even if it meant losing their lives in the process. My hope was that we would find them and eventually work together to take back the town.

One of the cops rushed down the hall and into an office. When he came out he was jangling some keys. He led us down into the basement to a locked room. After trying several keys he finally unlocked it. Inside the armory on one side of the wall were several Glocks, tactical shotguns, two MP5/10 submachine guns and three Colt AR-15s.

"Were you thinking of starting a war?"

"It's what SWAT used. We rarely used them."

I nodded and carried them out. As I watched these two officers go about loading the weapons and slipping into SWAT clothing, I couldn't help feel a wave of guilt about not pulling that trigger sooner. If I had maybe their two friends would have been here too.

"I'm sorry for your loss."

"What?"

"The two officers."

Officer McCabe responded with a sideways glance.

"Nothing you could have done, kid."

I wasn't sure if should have told them. Who knew how they would respond. Everyone was walking a thin line. Stress levels were high and well, I figured it wasn't the best time. Police officers were a tight-knit community. In many ways they were family. They spent hours in their cruisers together, and often spent more time with each other than their own spouse or kids. It wasn't a job as much as it was a career that didn't end even when they came home.

"Anything I can do to help?"

"Yeah, you know how to load a gun?"

I nodded. He then glanced down at the Glock in my hand.

"Load these up."

He went back into the room and came out holding a few canisters that I assumed were flashbangs. He filled a duffel bag with various boxes of ammo and then tossed the strap over his shoulder. The other officer glanced at me while he was checking a shotgun.

"You're that Frost kid. The one that's always getting in trouble. How come you aren't out with them?"

"I'm not one of them."

"You might want to dress differently then. You are

liable to get yourself shot."

"Point taken." I pressed bullets against the spring inside the magazine.

"By the way, I'm Hauser and that's McCabe."

"Yeah, I remember you."

They continued filling up two bags with as much as they could. I helped lug one upstairs. In the main office, Murphy was sitting on a desk with his shirt off. Shaw was bandaging him up. On the counter was a pile of bloodied cloths and a bowl of water. Murphy glanced at me.

"Sam," he motioned with his head.

I dropped the bag and went over. "Wanted to thank you for what you did back there. Took a lot of courage. I know it wasn't easy."

I shrugged. What was I meant to say to that?

"You said the second month would be hard."

He smirked. "That I did."

Across the room Billy, Luke and Corey were looking out the window. Luke had a cigarette in his mouth. I walked across to check out what they were staring at.

"Those little bastards are out there. I just saw two of them go up the side of that building," Luke said.

"It's like an infestation of rats."

"How's your back, Frost?" Luke asked with a smug grin.

Billy frowned. "Did we miss something? What happened?"

"I only saved his ass from two baldies. Didn't I?" He slung his arm around my neck and pulled me in as though everything we had just been through was some realistic video game.

"The look on that guy's face when I put a bullet through his skull. Priceless."

He took a deep drag on his cigarette and returned to looking out the window.

"What was it like?" Billy asked.

"What, killing?"

"Yeah."

"Didn't you kill anyone out there?"

Corey laughed. "He was too busy pissing his pants."

"Fuck you, fat boy," Billy replied.

There was a pause.

"I'll tell you what it was like. It was like that feeling you get after you've ejaculated. You know that initial head rush, and then a deep sense of satisfaction. Yeah, that's what it was like," Luke said.

"That was someone's kid," I said.

All three of them turned and looked at me. "What? Don't tell me you give a shit about that scumbag's life? You were a hairline away from him putting a cap in your ass. Hell, if I hadn't shown up there, who knows what they would have done to you."

"I'm just saying. Killing them isn't something to revel in."

"Oh grow a pair, Frost. Do you think they would have spent even a second thinking about your sorry ass if they had killed you?" He let out a laugh and shook his head.

"It doesn't matter. I'm just saying."

"Screw you and your self-righteous attitude. We are in a war."

I could tell he was enjoying it. Were some military personnel like that? I figured it took all kinds. There would always be the ones that signed up for the military just so they could kill people. Even though I imagined they were far and few between, there was bound to be a couple in every intake. I could see Luke being one of them. He would have been the kind of guy that would have killed an entire family and not missed a second of sleep, while others would have been tortured by the horror of what they had done.

"In fact, if I make it out of this, I'm thinking of signing up. I think I've found my calling."

All three of us looked at him like he was insane. Here he was dressed in black, looking like an emo and now he was ready to join the military? I shook my head and walked away.

Murphy hopped down off the table, rolled his shoulder a few times and grimaced.

"Don't you go pushing yourself, you hear me?" Shaw said as she picked up the rest of the bloodied rags and took them out into another room. I kind of figured that getting shot wasn't something that he was too bothered by. The guy was as tough as nails. If that had been any one of us, we would have laid out waiting for death to take us.

Officer Hauser came up the stairs carrying one of the duffel bags. He was in the middle of telling Murphy what they had gathered together when a bullet struck him in the neck, and he collapsed into Murphy's arms.

"Get down!"

What followed next was a series of rounds that shattered all the windows and peppered the walls. I watched as shards of glass rained down covering Luke, Corey and Billy. Brett had gone to the washroom when it happened. Each of us didn't dare move as the torrent of bullets continued for several minutes. By the time it stopped the station walls were like Swiss cheese. The first to move was McCabe who came up the stairs and slid an AR-15 over to Shaw, he then did the same with me. I looked down at the weapon like it was hot molten metal.

I'd never used one before. Another series of rounds erupted and tore through the station. I slid across the ground behind a large desk and backed up against it.

Murphy moved over and in a matter of ten seconds told me how to operate it. I kind of figured they didn't give it to me because they wanted to, they did it out of necessity. I mean, how hard could it be? I had fired an AK47. Shaw slid over to check on Hauser but he had stopped breathing. Beside him a pool of blood eased out. Only minutes ago I had been talking to him, and now he was dead. The thought that it could have been any one of us laying there made my pulse speed up.

"You guys okay?" Murphy asked.

Luke gave the thumbs-up. The next few minutes were spent arming the other three with semi-automatics. The look on Luke's face was as if he'd been given a car for his eighteenth. I was starting to wonder if such firepower should have been in any of our hands.

Silence followed the next wave of attack. Up until that point we hadn't returned fire. I figured Murphy knew what he was doing. He and McCabe moved into different spots around the office area. A glass window that had separated the police office from the general public waiting room was shattered, along with the windows in the front doors. From my position below the desk I could see movement near the doorway. A skinhead approached fast and then tossed in a Molotov cocktail. A sudden burst of flames erupted as the liquid coated the waiting room floor.

"They are trying to smoke us out," Corey shouted.

"You think?" Billy said getting up from his position and racing across the room even though Murphy was yelling for him to get down. Billy fired towards the front door and then dived into the corridor.

"Cover me." Officer McCabe rushed over to a fire extinguisher on the wall and ripped it off. He went outside the doors that separated the main office from the waiting room. A series of shots rang out. A few blasts from the extinguishers, white dust filled the room and the floor fire was soon dying down.

"Murphy."

He crouched down behind a wall and waited for Murphy to arrive. They then tried to heave a large cabinet full of awards and pieces of police history into position by the door to block any further attempts to burn us out. Seeing they were having trouble, I got up and scrambled over there. Brett followed suit while the others provided cover. Once all four of us got our backs into it, we shifted the steel and glass cabinet across the vinyl floor and covered the main entrance. We could hear bullets pinging off the back of it as we collapsed on the floor, exhausted. Shaw came down with another fire extinguisher and finished off what remained of the fire. The vinyl floor was bubbling black and letting off a foul smoke that was beginning to make us choke.

I coughed hard and McCabe led us out back to what was used as a garage for both the police and fire service. It was a fair size. The garage doors were made of steel. With all of us inside, he locked the door and we settled in for the night.

All of us were coughing and spluttering. Corey was snorting snot out of his nose to the disgust of Billy. Luke was fondling the M4 as though it was some new kind of sex toy. Shaw and Murphy sat off to one side with McCabe discussing how we were going to get out of this. Brett looked worried. No doubt he was thinking about Jodi. We had no idea where the others were or if they were even alive. I got up to go look for some water, my throat was parched and I had this hacking cough that made me feel like I was about to chuck up a lung.

"You don't think they can get in here?"

"If they want to, anything is possible. But it's not going to be easy. No one would be stupid enough to try and force their way in without giving thought to being shot."

"How are we going to do this?" Corey asked. "I mean, I'm so friggin' tired."

"My daughter is out there, I'm not sleeping until I know where she is."

McCabe took a hold of Murphy's arm. "So is my

family but we aren't going to be any good out there if we are tired. I know you think you are still one of the elite, Murphy but it's been three years since you got out. Even the best get tired."

Murphy sighed.

"We will rotate in shifts. Shaw and myself will take the first one. The rest of you should get some shut-eye."

I found a water tap on the far side of the building. I twisted the top and it gushed out clear. I cupped some of it in my hands and tossed it over my head and around my neck. The cold awakened my senses that were beginning to tire. As I took a drink, Brett came up behind me and placed his hand on my back.

"You okay, son?"

I didn't think I would ever get used to hearing that word — son. It was foreign to me. Though I had heard it many times over the course of seventeen, almost eighteen years it still didn't sit right with me.

I shrugged. "You?"

He sighed. "I will be when I find Jodi and this is over."

"You think it will ever be over?"

"There are a lot of military offshore and other countries will try to help."

"But with the fallout, the grid down and not knowing how many cities they hit. I can't see anyone risking his or her life to help. Besides, it could be weeks, maybe months before we see anyone up this way."

"Possibly."

Brett took a few gulps of water and then took a seat.

As we sat there I turned to him and watched him pull out a photo of Jodi and myself. The people at Children's Aid had taken it the day they brought me home. I was fifteen at the time. I didn't realize that he carried it around in his wallet.

"You kept that?"

He nodded. "I hope you know we didn't send you with Murphy because we didn't want you around. It's because we want this to work."

I nodded.

"Try to get some shut-eye."

As we tried to get comfortable, it was hard to fall asleep when outside I could hear gunfire. Was it Ally and her mother? Was Jodi still alive? I only hoped they were safe. I pushed the negative thoughts from my mind, if only for a few minutes.

TRIGGER HAPPY

Morning didn't arrive the way I imagined it would. We didn't enjoy a full night of rest. I was up before light broke. We maybe got four hours between us all. Several times over the course of the night the skinheads had tried to breach the inside of the station. They had managed to knock over the steel-shelving unit that we had shifted across the front of the door but none of them entered. It was scare tactics. Several times we had to go back out into the office and return fire.

In the early hours, just after five according to my watch, we decided to head out. Our aim was to find the others and then figure out a plan of action from there. Hauling two bags of ammo, we knew it was going to slow us up.

Outside Murphy told us to grab as much as we could carry without it weighing us down and then the rest would be stored in a dumpster down one of the alleys. All of us were wearing bulletproof vests that we had taken from the station. Chances of us surviving were slim at best, but at least this would offer us some form of protection.

Murphy waved us forward and we shuffled in the dark as a deep orange sun began to peek over the horizon. In the town the sound of gunfire had become less frequent. It wouldn't stay that way. To the north of us was I-90, and to the south residential homes. Unsure of which way they might have gone we separated into two groups. Murphy took myself, Corey and Billy with him while Luke went north with Shaw, Brett and McCabe.

"McCabe, come in," Murphy spoke into the comms unit.

"We're here."

"When this is over, you owe me a beer."

He chuckled on the other end. "Murphy, I'll buy you a case."

We moved quietly as one unit through the streets, only communicating with hand signals or whispers. Our group went down Residence Street and then over to Pearl looking for any signs of life. We entered some of the homes and checked. Some contained the dead bodies of those who had put up a fight and had been shot or hacked to death. Some homes had their front doors sealed shut and we saw mattresses on the other side. We assumed scared survivors barricaded themselves in.

Murphy knocked and moved out of the way expecting the occupants to shoot as there were a few bullet holes in the wood and the glass was shattered.

"Sara," he hollered through the open glass. When there was no answer we moved on. We worked our way from house to house by climbing over the yard fences and avoiding the main streets.

"You still got that knife on you?"

"No."

"I'm nearly out of ammo on this handgun."

I reached into my pocket and handed Billy fifteen bullets. We reached a house where the back door was open. It was dark inside but not nearly as bad as it was at night. The light from the morning sun was beginning to reveal what acts of violence had been committed. I was about to step inside when Murphy pulled me back. In a hushed voice he told me to wait. He crouched down and lifted up what I would have stepped on. Below a layer of towels was a huge slab of wood with nails protruding upwards like upright fingers.

"The owner?"

"That's my guess." He looked around nervously. "Let's leave this one."

"You think they're still inside?"

"If they are, they are probably twitchy and liable to shoot first."

Our town was known for having a few preppers. Like most towns in rural places, we had our fair share of hunting stores. One was owned by Kip Thorne, a grumpy old-timer who always managed to make local news for some new contraption that he'd built in preparation for World War Three. I had to wonder if he was still alive. His store was on the west side of town and to reach it, it would have meant wading our way through a shitload of skinheads. More than likely they had already cleaned the store out of supplies.

"No way, Kip will still be alive. That old bastard would have sealed himself in that vault of his," Billy said. "My old man took me in there to get some fishing lures this one time. He showed it to us."

"Oh yeah, what did it look like?"

He screwed up his face as though I was an idiot. "Like a vault. It was down in his basement. At first I thought he was taking us into a safe. You know, one of those big ass vaults you see in banks. It was like that. I think it was a panic room. Inside it had all these monitors and shit, a room connected to it with more canned food and another with an arsenal of guns. If anyone is going to survive this, it will be that fucker."

Murphy wasn't paying any attention; he moved with precision keeping his weapon shouldered like he was about to clear a house with a platoon of men.

"So what do you think, Murphy, how are we doing? I

bet you didn't expect us delinquents to survive this far."

"Stay quiet or this might be your last day alive."

Billy snorted and we pressed on checking out the next house. This one we entered. Every step we took was made with caution. Our eyes scanned for potential booby traps or an attack by someone who thought we were skinheads. The chances of us being killed by skinheads were high. But realistically it was more likely that a homeowner would shoot us. Everyone in the town would have been living in fear.

Murphy opened the French doors on the next house and we filed in behind him. He would signal for one of us to check one room while he checked another. As we entered the living room he threw up his hand. He mouthed the word *wait*. I couldn't see who was in there but he didn't want us to enter. I peered around the doorframe just in time to see him place the barrel of the M4 against the forehead of a skinhead who was asleep. Two more were sitting in chairs.

"Don't even breathe," Murphy said in a hushed voice.

It was enough to wake the guy. His eyes opened real wide. Billy filed past me even though I had told him to wait. That guy didn't listen to anyone. He aimed his gun at the other two.

"Slowly, slide onto the floor with your face down."

While he was instructing them I had my eyes on the stairs. If they were sleeping in the living room, were the bedrooms full?

"You are fucked," the skinhead said. I motioned to Corey that I was going to check upstairs. He followed. Now stairs at the best of times were creaky, even in new houses. I don't know what it was about stairs and me but I always found the one that was faulty. I hugged the wall with my back as I took one step at a time. As I kept my AR-15 raised and steady we ascended the steps. Now there was a strong possibility that we might have reached the top without any issue if it wasn't for one of the skinheads shouting in the living room. What followed next was a gun going off. I could only assume it was Billy's as Murphy would have wanted to keep everything quiet.

The next thing heard were multiple boots hitting the floor. I stepped back readying myself for them to come around the corner when Corey just opened fire straight through the ceiling above him. I heard a body thud, and then I found myself engaged as a skinhead rounded the corner with an AK47 in his hand. I unleashed a flurry of rounds while moving backwards. Cory was shooting upwards in a random pattern hoping to take out whoever else was trying to get to the stairwell. I was so focused on firing and trying not to be hit that I missed a step and fell backwards crashing into Corey and toppling down the four steps we had climbed. We landed hard but there was no time to get off Corey, I just kept my finger on the trigger until the skinhead collapsed.

Then there was silence.

"You want to get off me?" Corey muttered. For once I was glad that he was large. Had that been Billy I would have probably snapped his small frame. I rolled off and clambered to my feet. Murphy came out of the room forcing Billy forward.

"Hey, if I hadn't shot him he would have put a bullet in the back of your head. You can thank me later."

Murphy didn't reply; he just slid by him to make sure we were okay. He glanced up the stairs and saw the one skinhead hanging over the banister. Blood dripped from his mouth to the ground below.

"Any of you hurt?"

I shook my head.

"Just a little shaken up."

"This is one hell of a gun," Corey said admiring it with awe.

"You guys need to listen to me." He stared at Billy.

"Oh right, blame me."

"Billy, I'm not dicking around here. You make one mistake and all of us could end up dead."

Billy's chin dropped and he cast a glance back into the room where the dead skinheads lay bleeding out.

"Let's get out of here now. We have probably woken up half the town."

Corey nudged Billy on the way out the door and chuckled. Billy scowled at him. These two were always looking for a way to one-up the other. Idiots, but they were idiots that I was going to have to rely on if we wanted to survive this.

We pressed out into the warmth of the sun expecting that the day ahead of us would be filled with more surprises and horror.

RETRIEVAL

"Now what?" Corey said. "This place is going to be crawling with skinheads." Murphy got on the radio to check in with McCabe.

"Any sign of them?"

The radio crackled.

"Not so far. You?"

"Just a few."

We kept moving through the neighborhood going house to house. Though now we were even more cautious than before. We had cleared eight and found several dead bodies. The violent nature of those that murdered was becoming even more evident. They weren't just into shooting people but inflicting pain and at times humiliating them. Some of the dead were covered in feces, and the smell of urine was strong. Others had their hands tied, and their faces mutilated before being stabbed to death. Old, young, it didn't matter to them. It was a pack mentality and like savage wolves who were starving, they tore their victims apart while leaving a bloody trail behind them.

"You think we should pair off? We could cover more ground."

"No, it's too dangerous," Murphy said. "We stick together."

"I'm starving."

"The next house we enter, see what you can find, but make it quick."

The door was slightly ajar on the next home. As with the previous houses Murphy went in first. Once clear we entered the kitchen and began rooting around the cupboards for anything to eat. Corey grabbed up a box of cereal and scooped handfuls into his mouth then washed it down with water. Billy found five cans of peaches. He tore the tops open and devoured them while I searched inside the fridge. It smelled a little. It wouldn't take long before all the food in the stores would expire, then what? We hadn't even had a chance to think about the basics.

We lived from moment to moment fully expecting to be attacked.

"Do you think they'll eventually move on once they see their group dwindling?" Billy asked.

"No," Murphy said. "Being as they went to great lengths to kill a shitload of people, I expect they are ready to die if need be. They are in this for the long haul."

Billy scooped a few fingers into a can. Peach juice dripped down the side of his mouth.

"So are we going to have to kill them all?"

Murphy scoffed. "I hope not."

I slammed the fridge closed feeling frustration at the entire situation. We were nothing but puppets being led around by the nose. For the first time since this had started I was beginning to see how war could change a person. The lack of sleep, the hunger, the moments of terror and the images of horror could send a person over the edge. And we had just begun.

"A month, I don't think I could handle another week," I said.

Murphy kept an eye on the corridor. "You'll adjust. Right now you're not used to this. Your mind is telling you one thing. It will soon settle down."

"You make it sound like an addiction."

He chewed off a piece of bread that had been sitting on the counter. It was stale and there was even some funky purple fur growing on the side of it, however, it didn't seem to faze him.

"That's because it is an addiction. You have spent the last seventeen years of your life on a diet of ease. Warm beds, hot showers, an abundance of food, more technology than you know what to do with it. Pull away from all of that and your mind doesn't know what to do."

"Are you telling me you didn't have a cellphone?"

"No, I did but I wasn't attached to it the way some folks are. It's all about balance. People don't know what to do with themselves if you take away their gadgets and toys. That's because their identity is intrinsically wrapped up in that next email, that next post, that next... fill in the blanks."

Suddenly, Murphy tossed the bread on the ground and got a real serious look on his face.

"Get down and stay quiet."

We didn't argue with him. We dropped down and listened intently. What had he seen or heard? He signaled for us to back away from the kitchen opening. There was a moment of silence then we heard a door creak open and glass crunch beneath shoes. Whoever it was, there was more than one of them. All four of us had our weapons aimed at the doorway to the kitchen. The footsteps got closer. The moment I saw a leg come into view I pushed Billy's gun down.

"Sara?"

"Murphy."

We all got up and Sara hugged Murphy. Behind her were two of the older women that I'd seen from City Hall.

"Where's Ally?"

"I don't know. It all happened so fast. We heard three knocks at the back door of City Hall and thought it was you guys, when we opened all chaos broke out. There were three skinheads. We managed to kill one of them but the other two ran off. We assumed they would come back with others so we ventured out hoping to find you guys or another place to hide. Then we ran into more of them and somehow we got separated."

She had tears in her eyes when she was recalling what had taken place.

"Where did you last see her?"

"In the west end over on King Street." Sara looked around. "Where are the others?"

"They are north of here."

Murphy got on the radio. "McCabe."

He came on the line. "Go ahead."

"We have found Sara and a couple of others. Seems the rest are in the west end. You might as well work your way back down. We'll meet up at the Stardust Motel." When he got off the radio he motioned for us to get going.

"What about your daughter?"

"I'm going down there, I want you guys to keep an eye on Sara."

"No, let us do this. Take Sara back."

"Are you joking?" Murphy said to me.

"I get it, Murphy. Trust me. I'll take Corey and Billy. We'll be there and back before you know it. Besides," I glanced over to the older women, "they'll just slow us down."

"Let them do it," Sara said. It was clear that she was terrified.

He cast a glance at them, looked at us for a minute or two and then handed us the radio. "Be sure to stay in contact. You understand?"

"We're not dumb," Billy said.

Corey chuckled and Billy jabbed him in the side with his elbow

With that said, Murphy led Sara and the two women out the door. Murphy handed Sara a Glock and she just released the magazine, checked it and slapped it back in as though she had been around guns all her life.

We waited until they were gone before we ventured out. Threading our way through backyards, we decided to head into the forest that surrounded the town. It would make it easier to get across to the west side without being spotted. I focused on the trail ahead of us while Corey kept his eyes on the left and Billy focused on the right.

"What do you think they will do to her if they already have her?"

"Shut up, Billy," I said.

"Just saying."

"Yeah, for once keep your mouth closed."

"Whatever."

The forest floor was thick with vegetation. It was like wading through a green river. All that could be seen for miles were pine trees. In the local museum there were photos that dated way back to the time of silver mining. Mount Pleasant just looked like a speck among the surrounding greenery. If a plane went down it would take people weeks to find it, and that was if they were lucky. The forest was as dense as it was vast.

King Street ran south away from the town, then merged with Placer Creek Road. When we reached the edge of the trees and could see the homes, all three of us had our game faces on. It was quiet, we weren't sure if that was a good thing or not.

I dashed across the street and took cover behind an RV. I kept my hand raised and then motioned for the other two to join me once the coast was clear. King Street had homes on either side along with small apartment blocks. We began at the corner of High Street and worked our way down.

"I say we split up. There's too many. At least we stand a better chance of finding her and the others."

"There's only three of us."

"So I'll go alone," Billy said acting all confident.

I shook my head. "No, we need to stick together. Like Murphy said."

"Murphy ain't here."

"More reason to stick together," I said.

Billy scowled. "Who put you in charge?"

"I'm older than you, dick."

"What, by a year? Big deal."

"Well, five years if we take your mental age," Corey said.

I chuckled.

"I'm out of here." With that Billy double-timed it across the road.

"Go with him."

"No, if he wants to go by himself and get shot, let him."

"Corey."

He sighed and dashed across the road. When they were out of view I entered an apartment block. It wasn't big. There were two apartments on the second floor that could only be reached by stairs on the outside of the building. Inside there were five apartments. There was no doubt about it, I was taking a big risk going in there by myself. For all I knew it could have been full of skinheads still asleep. I slung the AR-15 around my back and took out the Glock. I went to the first door and turned the handle ever so slightly. It was locked. I repeated the same with the next. The third door opened. It made a slight creak. Inside it was dark, humid and smelled musty. The curtains were drawn. The smell was atrocious. I placed a hand over my mouth and kept my gun close to the side of my body. All I could make out was the silhouette of furniture. It was a single bachelor pad with one bedroom, a washroom and a kitchen that joined the living room. I could vaguely make out the shape of two people on the couch. I shuffled over to the curtain and eased it back, just enough to get a better view.

I wished I hadn't.

Hunched over on the couch were two adults in their early forties. The man had both of his eyes removed and his throat slit. The woman's clothes had been torn from her body and she was slumped over the end of the couch with her naked rear end facing upward. I didn't even want to dwell on what they had done to her. Both weren't moving.

Horrified, I exited there quickly, trying to push the

images of depravity from my mind. Outside the sun cast its warm light down. I went house to house checking for survivors. By the looks of things people had fled as most of the homes were abandoned.

The sixth property had people inside. If the teenage son hadn't recognized me, I was sure my brains would have been all over the floor. I had entered and silence permeated the house. I was in the middle of checking the fridge when I felt the cold gun barrel pressed against the back of my head.

"Put the gun on the ground and don't look around."

"Okay, okay. Don't shoot. I'm not here to start trouble."

"Yeah, that's why you have been killing people in our neighborhood."

"You've got it wrong. That wasn't me."

"Don't bullshit me, boy."

"I swear."

I went to turn my head and he smacked me hard with the butt of his gun. I fell to the floor.

"I told you. Don't look around."

"Dad, I know him."

I looked up and saw a kid by the name of Tom Barrington. He was a jock in the school. One of those kids who spent all his time on the football field and talking about the latest game.

"Tom?"

He crouched down and helped me up.

"I don't care whether you know him. Look at him. He's one of them."

"Sir, I swear. I know how this looks but…"

"Dad, he got sent away to Murphy's camp."

"Murphy? Do you know where he is?"

"He was the one that sent me to find his daughter."

They helped me to a seat and got a cloth for the cut on the side of my face. I brought them up to speed on what occurred.

"Bastards took my wife. I haven't seen her. She wasn't with your group, was she?"

"She might be there. There were a number of people at

City Hall. I don't know all of them."

Despite it being a small town, I didn't know everyone in it. I'd only been there two years. But in that time it seemed as if my reputation preceded itself but for all the wrong reasons. Tom's father didn't trust me. He kept his gun on me while I downed a glass of water.

"Look, all I can say is it's probably best to hang tight where you are. There are others in the town fighting back. We've heard them but who knows how many have died."

"Do you know how this happened?"

"Not exactly."

"What do you mean? You are one of them."

Tom's father grabbed my wrist that had the tattoo of the swastika.

"It was a mistake." I yanked my wrist away.

"Really? Funny how you say that now that you have a gun pointed at your head."

"Oh, Dad, give it a rest. He's not going to do shit." Tom looked at me. "Are you?"

"I need to go. I have to find Ally."

"We saw her."

"You did?"

"Last night. She was among a whole group that were being chased by them."

"And you didn't think to help?"

"There was nothing we could do. They've been killing people in the middle of the streets. I watched my neighbor get his head stomped. I've already lost my mother."

"She might still be alive, just hiding. Which way did you see them go?"

Tom pointed.

I got up and Tom's father reluctantly handed my guns back. As I made my way to the back door, Tom's father spoke. "Hey, kid, I'm sorry about your head."

With my head throbbing I started heading south. I was about to head into a residence when I heard a whistle. I turned to see Billy on the other side of the road. He gestured as if to say they hadn't found them. I had cleared two houses before I came to the old people's residence. A one-story red brick building with the doors covered in spray paint. Some of the wire-meshed windows had been busted out. I hesitated wondering whether to go in or not.

As I got closer to the door I saw dry blood covering the handle. I pulled it back and noticed even more blood covering the ground. It looked as though someone had been dragged inside. Cautiously I stepped in and made sure to not let the door bang behind me. It was dark inside, except for the areas where daylight seeped in. In the lobby was a front desk, a basement elevator off to the right and a waiting area. The floors were tiled and the carpets were flowery.

I tucked the Glock inside my waistband and pulled the rifle around. I had a bad feeling about this. I glanced back at the main entrance contemplating joining Corey and Billy across the street. I blew out my cheeks and pressed on. On the wall was an outline map indicating where the apartments, the laundry area and game room were. The whole place smelled like rotten cabbage and bedpans. I moved quickly down the corridor in a sideways motion so I could keep an eye on both ends of the corridor. Every time I opened a new door, I had this sinking feeling in my stomach that the next one would have someone with a gun behind it.

After checking six rooms I was starting to think that the entire town had upped and left. Then it dawned on me. We had been away in the wilderness when the terror attacks had started. Was it possible that many of the people had left town after the power went down but before things kicked off? I shook my head. No, maybe younger families might have retreated but not the elderly. Where could they have taken them?

I was inside a room when I heard voices. Whoever it was went right past the room I was in. Laughter broke out and then the sound of a can being kicked over.

"Give me the cigarettes."

"You should have seen the look on her face when I told her she was going to be spending the night with me."

"So how was it?"

"Oh, she wrestled a little but I actually think she got into it in the end."

I pulled the door back ever so carefully. I peered out between the crack and couldn't see anyone. Right then I heard their voices again as they walked back the other way. I closed the door and waited until they had gone by before looking out. Sure enough, there were two skinheads smoking in the main lobby. I waited until they disappeared around the corner before I ventured out. *Get the hell out of here,* I thought. My pulse raced faster. I rushed down the corridor and came around the corner. I had made it about halfway down the corridor when I heard more voices. I tried the next door but it was locked. I moved along and tried three more but those were locked. I couldn't believe it. Here I was about to go toe-to-toe in a retirement home.

As I shouldered the next door and it didn't open, I raised the rifle in preparation. That's when the door behind me opened. It happened so quickly, a hand went over my mouth and I stumbled backwards.

JACK HUNT

SHIVER

Caught off balance, all I could feel was a hand, the door closed and that's when I saw her. "Keep it down. They are everywhere."

"Ally."

"How the hell did you get in here without being seen?"

"I just used the main entrance." I cast a glance around the room. "Where are the others?"

"We all ran in different directions last night. My mother, have you—"

"She's with your father."

A look of relief washed over her face.

"Are you okay?"

"Why wouldn't I be?"

"Whatever," I said, walking into the room and looking around. It was basically a small apartment for an elderly couple. A simple living room, kitchen, bathroom and bedroom. The walls were covered in some flowery wallpaper. Red string hung from various places around the apartment. It was to be pulled in the event that someone fell.

Ally scowled. "What's that mean?"

"You are like your father. Oh forget it. I need to get you out of here."

She frowned. "You. Get me out of here?"

We waited a few minutes until the voices outside died down.

"How long have you been in here?"

"I've been moving around most of the night."

"Why not just go out the window?"

"Because I'm not leaving without Kiera."

"Kiera Shaw?"

"Yeah," she replied while she cracked the door a little to take a look.

"Kate Shaw. Officer Shaw's daughter?"

"Please tell me my father is nearby and he didn't send just you to find me."

"Actually he did. Well, Corey and Billy."

"That figures."

"You got a spare weapon?"

I pulled the Glock from my waistband and handed it to her. "You know how to—"

Before I could say anything she had released the magazine, checked it and reloaded.

"You were saying?"

"Do you know what room she's in?" I asked.

"No, we're going to have to check them all. They grabbed her though, I saw it happen."

Suddenly I thought about what that guy had said. Ally must have caught the change of expression.

"What is it?"

I breathed in. "I think I know which area she might be in."

A few minutes later we were making our way down the corridor. I retraced my steps back to the main lobby and crossed over to the next hallway.

"What room?"

"I don't know. I saw them head in this direction. One

of them said…" I trailed off.

"What is it?"

I was about to respond when we were spotted. The skinhead yelled. I grabbed Ally and we fled, heading towards an exit at the far end. I unloaded several rounds behind us as we kept running. The moment I shouldered the door, Ally hesitated while returning fire.

"What are you doing? Let's go!"

"I'm not leaving without her."

"It's too late."

"No."

"We'll come back."

I could see even more skinheads pouring out of doors. It was only a matter of time before a bullet hit us.

"Come on," I shouted, motioning for her to run because three more were coming down the side of the building.

We raced into the surrounding forest. My throat burned and my thighs protested as we tried to lose them. Running was like wading through thick mud. The forest floor was covered in veiny tree roots that protruded up, and massive amounts of evergreen plants and shrubs. Ally tripped and face planted. I hauled her up while shooting between the trees. I could see there were about ten of them fanning out.

The further we ran into the forest, the darker it got as branches spider webbed above a canopy that blocked out daylight. As we came over a rise, it suddenly dropped off and both of us stumbled down, rolling and picking up speed. If the AR-15 hadn't been attached to a strap I would have lost it for sure. I collided hard with the ground and came to a rest about forty feet down the steep incline. Ally was off to my left side. She was groaning. I put a finger up to my lips trying to get her to remain quiet.

I could hear them above us.

"Where did they go?"

"You see them?"

"Over this way."

Their boots pounded the forest floor and slowly

became distant. In that time I didn't move an inch. Once I was sure they were gone I crawled my way over. Every muscle in my body ached. My shirt was torn down the side and I had a gash on the side of my ribs. Breathing hurt, so I wasn't sure if I had broken a rib or not. When I got over to Ally, she was in an even worse state. Her dark hair was full of dirt and leaves. As I looked down at her leg I grimaced. There was a piece of branch sticking into her thigh.

"Just help me up."

"With that in you?"

"I'm not sitting here and bleeding out."

"Aren't we supposed to break it and leave the piece in you?"

"Just do it."

She placed a hand over her mouth and I looked at her briefly before I yanked hard. It was as sick as shit pulling it out. Now she had a wound on her right leg that was bleeding badly. I took off my shirt, tore a section, then wrapped it around her thigh and tied it.

"You think you can move?"

"I don't have a choice."

I put one of her arms around my shoulders and began hauling her up. She groaned loudly and I paused for a second to check. They were still in the forest. I could hear them shouting.

"We need to move fast."

"Follow the stream, that way."

I assumed she knew where she was going because I hadn't a clue. Everywhere we turned looked the same. Trees for miles. Dense vegetation and the sound of skinheads yelling. We stumbled further down the incline, sliding occasionally and a few times falling on our asses. When we made it to the bottom, we could see the stream, it lapped up against the banks. I was paranoid that at any minute they were going to jump us. But it never happened. We stumbled across the stream getting our clothes soaked in the process. We followed it on the other side of the bank for a mile or two before we took a break under a large oak tree. I removed the cloth around her leg and went down to the water and squeezed out the blood. I soaked it good, squeezed the excess and reapplied it. Looking around the forest I saw a plant that had large leaves. I went over and snapped one off, I used it as a cup to collect water and give it to Ally. She drank it down fast.

"You think you can keep going?"

She nodded and I helped her back up. The last thing I wanted was to be found outside. There was no telling how long they would search for us. After killing one of the men back at the home for the elderly, it was certain they would be hunting us for a while. We pressed on downstream away from the town. How long we walked, I'm not sure. When Ally said she couldn't go any further, I placed the rifle in her hands because she had lost the Glock in the fall.

"I'll be right back."

I registered the fear in her eyes. There had to be a home nearby. We were close to the main road that led into Mount Pleasant. I dashed through the forest until I came across two cabins in the distance. I crouched down behind large plant life and spied on the property for a few minutes before approaching. Circling around back, I looked through the dirt stained window. There was no movement. I tried the back door. It was locked. I used my elbow to break the glass and reached inside. Once I was certain that no one was in any of the rooms, I returned for Ally. She was jumpy when I arrived, thinking I was one of them.

Once we made it to the cabin, I barricaded the door with a large wooden cabinet and then used a table to do the same for the front door. I fished around inside the cupboards for a first-aid kit. I found some clean bandages. There was no lotion or anything that might have helped me clean the wound. Inside a drawer was a pair of scissors. I returned to the living room and began cutting up the pant leg.

"Hey, don't go too high."

The wound looked nasty, but once I got some water on it and wiped away some of the dirt, it didn't seem too bad. It was going to hurt for some time but she'd live. I went and looked around an office, and then in the living room. It was sparse, partially furnished and lacked a woman's touch. That's when I found a bottle of bourbon. I used it to clean the wound. Ally grimaced as I poured it on her leg. She then grabbed it from me and took a swig.

"I think you should be okay. Just a flesh wound," I remarked with a faint smile.

She studied me as I leaned back and tried to catch my breath. We sat there in the quiet occasionally glancing at one another.

Ally took another swig. "So how did you end up at my father's program?"

"A pissed-off judge and an equally pissed-off foster parent."

She smirked. "No, I mean what did you do?"

"I was caught with drugs. They got me for intent to sell."

"Were you? Selling, I mean?"

"Yeah. Though to be fair they weren't mine. I was doing a favor for a friend."

She nodded and offered me the bottle. I took it and chugged back the amber liquid. It felt like fire going down my throat. I was more into drinking beer than spirits. I got up and went over to the window to check if there was anyone outside. Satisfied that there was no one I sat back down.

"That tattoo on your wrist."

I glanced at it making a mental note to get it removed if I ever made it out of this mess.

"What about it?"

"They make you do that too?"

"No, I did that on my own accord. I kind of wish I hadn't now."

"But you didn't know about what they were going to do, did you?"

"No. This is as much a shock to me as it is to anyone else."

"But didn't they talk about this?"

"No. I mean, they talked about taking back the country but I didn't think it meant this. They don't share everything with you."

"Just the stuff that gets you in trouble."

"Yeah, something like that."

I took another swig from the bottle then handed it to her. She was shivering.

"I'll go get us some towels."

Our clothes were soaked through from falling into the stream. I returned a few minutes later and handed over one. I dried off my hair and she looked at me.

"A little privacy?"

My eyebrows rose. "Sure."

The living room had French doors. I pulled them together and changed out of my clothes, dried off and then rooted around the rooms for something I could wear in the meantime. The cabin must have belonged to a hunter. All I could find was camouflage tops, plaid shirts and zero pants.

"Any luck?" Ally asked.

I opened the door partially and caught a glimpse of her. She had her top off and was hugging her breasts with one arm. I stood there for a second and swallowed hard.

"Are you just going to stand there and gawk?"

"Sorry. Um. Here you go." I tossed her a shirt.

VISITORS

It would take a while for our clothes to dry and time wasn't something we had. "How did you manage to survive last night?" I asked. I was still puzzled at the fact that she had managed to escape the skinheads even though she had stayed the entire night in the same residence that some of them had slept in.

"I told you. I hid. When they went door to door checking the rooms I pushed up the ceiling tiles and stayed there until they left."

"Resourceful." I looked down at the ripped jeans. "You should probably take them off."

"I bet you would like that, wouldn't you?"

I smirked. "I didn't mean it like that. Besides that's the last thing on my mind."

"Really?"

I turned my eyes away from her and went over to the window thinking I heard something outside. A wind blew the leaves. I thought I saw movement in the tree line but there was nothing.

"We should really go back."

"You are in no state to be going back to the residence."

"Kiera is there by herself."

"I understand but everyone is in the same predicament. Hiding, running. We don't know how many of them are inside that building. I shouldn't have even gone in there by myself."

"Why didn't you bring others with you?"

"I did, they were across the road checking other homes." I stared at her for a second and she looked as if she was becoming self-conscious. "Have you eaten anything?"

She shook her head. I nodded. "Okay, I'll see what I can find."

I went back out into the kitchen and started looking through the cupboards for canned goods. There were canned beans and soup. Without some way to cook them they would taste pretty nasty but it was all we had. I checked the drawer for a can opener and returned to the living room. Ally was wearing these skinny jeans, a large section was torn where I had ripped them to get at the wound and bandage it up. She had pulled them down and was examining the wound. Her ass was the first thing I saw when I came in. She whipped around and got this embarrassed look on her face.

"Nothing I haven't seen before," I said placing a can of beans down and opening it there. She grabbed at the towel and wrapped it around her waist.

"How come I never saw you with any girl?"

"What?"

"Before this."

I shrugged. "I haven't been here long enough to get to know any, and let's face it, I don't exactly fit with in with the crowd."

She took a seat across from me and began peppering me with questions about where I had grown up.

"How many foster homes have you been in?"

"Too many."

I handed her the can and a fork. She began scooping it out and eating fast as though she hadn't eaten for a week. She only slowed when she realized that I was looking. She chewed and swallowed hard.

"I never liked beans but I'm famished."

"Amazing how picky we get when everything is before us, isn't it?"

She nodded.

"Your father. What's the deal with him?"

"What do you mean?"

"When did he separate from your mother?"

"Three years ago."

"Why?"

She had a mouthful of food. She cleared her throat before answering. "My father had always been away with the teams. SEAL teams. We didn't really see him much and when we did he wasn't exactly there, if you know what I mean." She paused and began digging at the food in the can. "I guess my mother got lonely."

"And Matt?"

"Was an old work friend of my mother's. She's a nurse."

It dawned on me that I hadn't told her that Matt was dead. I wasn't sure how she would react so I decided not to say anything. We had enough on our plate as it was. The last thing she needed was more bad news. If we managed to get out of this I figured her mother would tell her.

"Why did your father leave the teams?"

"After my mother filed for divorce. He kind of went to pieces for a while. He said it was PTSD but I know him better than that. Besides, do you think anyone would have allowed him to get involved in a program helping others if they thought he was mentally unstable?"

I chuckled.

"Something amusing about that?"

"No. Just after what we went through in the past month in the wilderness, I'm pretty sure most would have said he was unstable."

She shook her head and the corner of her lip went up.

"That's more Dan than him." She finished up the can of beans and set it on a side table. Ally got up and hobbled a little over to where a fireplace was. She picked up a photo frame of an Indian family.

"Where do you think they went?" she asked.

I didn't answer her. I had caught something out the side of my eye. Movement by the window. At first I thought it was just blurred vision but when I saw it a second time I was certain it had been someone peering in.

"Ally." She turned around still holding the photo frame.

"Put the frame down, smile at me and then come over."

"What?"

"Just do as I say."

My eyes darted to the window and then back to her without moving my head. She must have understood as she laid the photo back down and shuffled over. We walked out into the corridor.

"Go upstairs. If you hear anything, get out the window

and run."

I went over to the back door where the large wooden cabinet was and tried to see if I could get a better look at who was outside. When I saw the door handle begin to turn I pointed for her to go. I readied the rifle and backed away. The door unlocked and whoever was on the other side pushed against it but the door just hit up against the cabinet.

I contemplated shooting through the door but without knowing who it was, I didn't want to risk killing an innocent. It was possible that someone else was looking for somewhere to hide. I moved back into the living room and went over to the window. They were gone. I was about to join Ally, when I heard the sound of a window being shifted up in the room across the hallway. I edged my way over to the French doors and pushed on aside. With my finger dancing near the trigger I felt my pulse race as I heard heavy boots hit the hardwood floor. I shouldered the rifle and prepared to fire. Whoever it was shuffled through the next room into the kitchen and began rummaging around in the cupboards.

I eased my way around the French door, then slowly approached. They were wearing a large anorak that covered them from their head to their knees.

"Slowly turn around," I said with the gun aimed at them from across the room. Their hands went up. Just as they began turning I heard a click right by my ear.

"Drop it."

Shit! I thought. I began bending at the knees to lower the gun when I saw who it was in the jacket. "Billy? Shit. I could have killed you."

"Sam."

I turned to find Corey behind me. "Surprise."

"You assholes," I replied grabbing up my weapon.

"Ah, it was his idea. He said it would freak you out. I borrowed the jacket from a house. Like it? By the way, where are your pants?"

I shook my head. "Drying off."

"Yeah I bet. Where is she?" Billy asked.

I hollered up the stairs. "Ally. It's okay, you can come

out." Her feet padded across the floor and then she came down. Billy's eyebrows rose. "Well damn, if I'd known you were getting it on, I would have left you to it."

Ally still had the towel wrapped around her waist and the shirt she was wearing was a little bit too big for her. The top buttons at the front were undone enough that Billy got a good shot of her cleavage.

"Don't be a dick." She brushed past him and he sniffed, smelling her hair like a freak. I scowled at him. A minute later she reappeared from the living room wearing the torn jeans.

"How did you know we were here?"

"We heard the gunfire and figured we should come and help."

"Oh, you figured that, did you?" Ally asked.

"What's the deal with her?" Billy asked thumbing at her but asking me. "Anyway, we saw you make a break for it into the forest."

I went over to the window and looked out. "Anyone follow you?"

"Do you really think we are that dumb?"

Corey didn't say anything. He went back into the kitchen and began looking for some food. I told him there were a few cans of beans left.

"Did you see where they went?"

"Yeah, they circled back around to the residence. Anyway, are we getting out of here?" Billy took out a packet of cigarettes and banged one out. He placed it between his lips and lit it then blew a big puff of grey smoke.

"Not until we get Kiera."

"Kiera Shaw?" Corey spun around looking vaguely interested.

She nodded.

"Where is she?" Corey asked.

"Back at the old people's residence."

"Oh fuck no, we aren't going back there," Billy said blowing more smoke out. "She's on her own."

Ally scowled at him. "No one asked you to help."

"Good, as I wasn't going to give it," he replied while

making his way into the living room and looking around.

"Don't listen to him, he's an ass," Corey said.

"Yeah, an ass that just saved yours."

"Please, you didn't save me."

Billy came wandering back into the kitchen looking all pleased with himself. "That skinhead was going to blow your head off. If it wasn't for my distraction you wouldn't have got the gun off him."

"You are full of it, Manning. I had it well under control," Corey replied rooting through the cupboard. He pulled out a wooden mop, placed it against the sink and snapped it in half. Meanwhile we looked on with curiosity. He reached under the sink, pulled out a can of wasp spray, then shook it up and down. He went through some drawers and pulled out some masking tape and began tucking it into his pocket.

"What are you planning on doing with all of that?" Ally asked.

"You ever seen the flame that this shit spits out?"

She shook her head.

"You might if any of those baldies show up."

"We're not going in there."

"Yes we are," Ally said.

Billy leaned against the counter. "No offense. I'd be glad to help but do you know if she's even alive? If they have her, I expect they've already had their way with her and killed her by now."

"Why do you immediately jump to a conclusion that they would do that?"

"Uh. Look around you. You think this is fucking Disneyland? They are savages. There are no cops to stop them and no one is coming to save us. They are going to do whatever the hell they like."

Ally scowled at him and hobbled back into the next room. I tossed Billy the bird and followed her.

"Pay no attention. He doesn't know what he's talking about."

"Would they do that?"

I remembered what I had heard one of them saying back at the residence. They didn't say her name but I kind of figured it was her.

"We just need to go and get her."

"Why are you dodging the question?"

I turned back. "I'm not."

"But you're one of them."

"What, because I shaved my head, and got a swastika tattoo?"

She raised an eyebrow.

"People are entitled to make bad life choices. I'm sure you've made some yourself."

With that I turned and went out of the room. I was getting a little tired of people thinking that I was one of them. Back in the kitchen the other two were still going on about some shit that I didn't care about.

"Grab your stuff, let's go."

"I'm not going in there," Billy said.

"No, you're not. You are going to take Ally back to her father. You still got the two-way?"

Corey reached into his bag and pulled it out and handed it to me.

"Come in, Murphy?"

The radio crackled.

"Go ahead."

"We've got your daughter. Where are you?"

He gave the address. "Is she okay?"

"Yeah, a bit cut up but she'll live."

"Cut up?" he shot back.

"Her leg is injured but I bandaged it up."

"Make your way back."

"Billy is going to bring her back. We are going in to get Kiera."

I heard Kate in the background say her daughter's name.

"Sam, did you say you've seen my daughter?"

I cleared my throat and looked at the other two guys before pressing the button. "Yeah."

"Is she okay?"

"We don't know, Kate, but we're going to get her."

Murphy got back on the line. "You need some help?"

"Of course, but you are there and we are here. Don't

worry about us, just do what you got to do."

When I got off the line, Billy was all up in my face.

"I'm not taking princess anywhere. And who the hell are you to give me orders?"

I grabbed a hold of him and threw up him against the wall. "Your mouth is going to get you in a lot of trouble. Just do what you're fucking told."

"Oh, what are you going to do, eh? You gonna beat me like your baldie friends out there?"

Corey placed his hand on my shoulder. "Just let it go, dude, he's not worth it."

Staring intently at him, I released my grip.

"Just because the world has gone to shit, it doesn't give you the right to act like an asshole," he said walking off.

"I can take her," Corey offered.

"No, I need someone with me who isn't going to run at the first sign of trouble."

"Do I have a say in the matter?" Ally appeared in the doorway.

I shrugged. "I just think it's best, with your leg and all,

that you head back."

She frowned and I got a sense that I had overstepped my boundary. "I'm not an invalid. I can help."

"No offense but you will slow us down."

She clenched her jaw and I saw her fist ball then release. She cast a glance at Billy and he smirked.

"Trust me, princess, I don't like this anymore than you do."

"So what's the plan?" Corey asked.

"Plan? There is no plan. You don't plan for stuff like this. You wing it and hope to god you get out of it alive." I turned back to Corey. "How many more of those cans are down there?"

"A shitload. They must have had one hell of an infestation problem."

He opened the cupboard and there were about ten cans.

"Toss them in a bag. I'm going to squeeze back into my wet pants."

BACK DOWN

We watched Billy and Ally stroll off into the distance. Billy offered to support her with his arm but she refused. I caught her mutter something about how she'd rather die.

Corey checked his ammo before we waded our way back through the forest towards the residence. My pants were still wet and I could feel them pinching my leg. It was the most uncomfortable feeling.

As we got closer to the residence we could see more of them outside. Not all of them were going house to house like they had been doing the day before, most seemed content to linger around drinking, playing heavy punk music using a generator and taking potshots at glass beer bottles. A non-stop party.

Markus Wainright was among them.

My mind drifted back to the first time I had got introduced to Markus. Six foot four, a Nazi eagle on his chest and a spider web that ran over his bald head, he looked as mean as he acted. And like most of them, if you got on their good side, they were as nice as ever.

He ran the local mixed martial arts gym in town. It originally started with backyard tournaments, then when more and more people showed up wanting to be trained, Mount Pleasant MMA was born. Of course he couldn't support himself on memberships alone. So his extracurricular activities such as selling drugs offset the losses from the gym. Not everyone who signed up for the gym became a skinhead. Some left after a couple of months because they couldn't handle the way they spoke about others in the town. Others couldn't take their hard-nosed attitudes or their lack of empathy for weakness. He observed those who came in over a period of a year. He only took on those who showed a taste for violence, were loyal and could be trusted. Most of his staff were convicted felons. They had done time for one thing or another.

I had been there six months when he approached me. I was in the middle of a sparring session when he stopped it and pulled me to one side.

"You've got a lot of heart, kid, but I notice you back away once your opponent is on the ground."

"Fight's over."

He shook his head and narrowed his eyes. "It's never over until they aren't moving."

That was the first time I got a sense of who I was dealing with.

"Look, let me show you. Nick, let's go."

Nick was sitting in his corner with his gloves on. He hesitated for a second and looked around at the others. The other six guys that were sparring in the room stopped and watched. They knew that whenever Markus got on the mat, they were about to watch a train wreck. I stepped back to give them room and they began.

At first Nick jabbed a few times and I could tell he was being cautious. Markus picked up on it too.

"Come on. Don't hold back."

That's when Nick got a few jabs in. Markus returned with a few punches and landed one that nearly knocked Nick on his ass. It was when Markus went for a right jab, Nick shot out of the way and landed a hard hook to the side of Markus's face, that he saw red. There was no hesitation. No thinking about what he was going to do. He turned and ran at Nick, slammed him twice in the face and then threw him into the wall. The guy landed in a heap and was trying to get up when Markus jumped on top of him and started pounding him in the face. Five, ten and then twenty punches later when his face was swollen and he was letting out a gargled breath, Markus stopped. Markus got off him and looked at me. He smiled a toothy grin that was covered in blood, then brought his foot up and brought it home on Nick's nuts. Nick didn't even respond.

He was placed in intensive care for several weeks. He never returned to the gym. No charges were filed against Markus as Nick never told the police how it happened. I later learned that he had a beef with Nick. Something to do with the way he had come on to his woman. That was a serious no go. Whether there was any merit to the rumor was neither here nor there. In that moment I knew that I wasn't dealing

*with someone that was just dangerous. I was dealing with
someone who enjoyed hurting others.*

*His comment after the fight was just four words. "Don't
ever back down."*

With that he disappeared out back.

I stared intently at him from the tree line.

Corey snapped his fingers in front of my face. "Sam.
Are you with me?"

I shook my head. "Yeah."

"Are we going in?"

I nodded slowly and we made our approach. At the
rear fire door we opened it and slipped inside. In the
corridor we made our way down to the first room and
tried the handle. It was open. I wanted to make sure that
if we needed to dive into a room, we at least knew which
rooms were unlocked. We did this with multiple rooms
on our way down the corridor.

"Where is she?"

"I think she's over in the east wing."

I remembered the map on the wall. We were on the

south side. As we made our way up the hall that took us closer to the east side, a door opened and a skinhead came out doing up his belt. He turned sharply to the right but he saw us in his peripheral vision. Before he could get a word out I slammed the butt of the gun in his face and knocked him to the ground. I followed through with three more sharp jabs and then motioned for Corey to open the door that the guy had just come out of.

I crouched down and slung my rifle behind my back. I fished around in his jacket and found a 9mm handgun. I snagged it up and tucked it into the back of my waistband.

Corey pushed the door open but instead of holding it he rushed inside. The door swung closed and I jumped up at the sound of a scuffle. I shouldered the door and entered. Lying motionless on the bed completely naked was Kiera. Corey was strangling a skinhead on the floor who had no pants on. I rushed over and then I saw who it was.

It was Tommy Black.

"Corey," I tried to pull him off but he just pushed me away.

"This fucker deserves to die."

Tommy was gurgling and trying to grab at Corey's face but he just kept leaning back.

"You're going to kill him, Corey."

As strange as it sounded, in that moment I felt torn. I knew Tommy. At least I knew the guy that had introduced me to the group. Right then Tommy managed to pry Corey's hands away and push him off him. I stood there frozen for a minute maybe two.

I had spent time with him. He was the only one who had treated me like a person from the time I had arrived in Mount Pleasant. Now Tommy was on top of Corey.

"Help," they both croaked out. My eyes flitted to Kiera on the bed. I shook my head, unable to comprehend what they had done. A second, maybe two and then I brought the butt of the gun against the side of Tommy's face. Once, twice and then a third time. He collapsed on top of Corey. Arms draped at his side.

Corey coughed hard. "What took you so long?"

I went over to Kiera. She looked as if she was in a comatose state. Her eyes were open and she was looking up at the ceiling. I threw a blanket over her naked body and untied her restraints.

Corey got up and gave Tommy a kick, twice.

"No time for that, help me with her. Get her clothes."

The moment I got one of her hand restraints loose, Kiera went ballistic. It was as though she snapped out of whatever world she had escaped to in order to handle what they were doing to her. She scratched my face and I let out a yell. Her legs were still restrained so was one of her arms. Corey tried to help but he only ended up with a smack in the eye.

"Kiera, it's me, Corey."

She didn't respond. She was jacked up on something, or running on pure fear.

"Corey, go lock the door."

While he went over I tried to calm her down and let her know that we were there to help. They had muzzled her with a rag otherwise I was certain she would have attracted attention. The only way I could get her to stop trying to scratch me was to put myself behind her and hold both of her arms. I kept repeating in her ear. "I'm not here to harm you. We're going to get you out."

Slowly but surely she stopped resisting and began crying.

"Corey, her clothes. Toss them over." I kept a firm grip as I slipped the top over her using one hand. Once we had her top half covered up, I released her slowly and backed away to see if she was going to go ballistic. Instead she just stared into the distance.

"You ready?"

I figured Corey knew the moment we untied her legs that there was a chance she would attack us. We couldn't tell if she realized we were there to help or if she thought we were planning on moving her to another room to continue whatever sexual acts they had done to her.

It was like releasing a tiger. There was no telling what she would do next.

Tommy groaned in the corner and Corey went over and slammed him as hard as he could in the face again with his gun. He slumped to the ground — out cold.

Once the final restraint was untied, Kiera didn't move. I handed her the skirt that was at the bottom of the bed but she didn't even look at it. It was if she had gone inside herself.

"Give me a hand."

The moment I tried to lay her back so Corey could get the skirt on, she went nuts.

"Hold her," Corey said as he attempted to get the skirt on without getting kicked in the face. If it wasn't for the fact that she was petite, I was pretty sure she would have battered us. Once her skirt was on I released her.

"Kiera. We're going to take you back to your mother."

Her eyes locked on to mine. "I need you to trust us. Can you do that?"

She hesitated, nodded and that was all I needed to see.

Outside in the hallway it was empty.

"Okay, let's go."

We shuffled out and filed down the corridor heading back towards the fire exit at the rear of the building. My nerves were on edge. Corey held on to Kiera's arm and went ahead while I turned back keeping an eye out. Rounding a corner, we were on the last stretch of corridor before the exit, when two skinheads came out of a room. I lifted my gun and they dived back inside the room. What followed next was a series of shots. I unloaded about eight rounds to prevent them from coming at me. While I was running backwards, I heard the door open and Corey and Kiera rushed outside.

What I didn't see because I was running backwards was a skinhead come out of the next corridor. He slammed me into the drywall almost breaking it. A few sharp jabs to the face and I was now fighting for my life. Out the side of my eye I could see the other two skinheads were out of the room and rushing down to help their pal.

The door swung open, a gun fired and the guy in front of me collapsed.

"Come on," Corey screamed. I fired a few rounds at the two who were coming up and hit one of them. The other one hit the ground out of fear. Rushing out the door, Corey slammed it closed and pushed a large BBQ in front of the door.

As we began running for the forest I heard my name called out.

"Sam."

I turned to see Markus Wainright.

"You are dead! You are a dead man."

Corey threw the bag of aerosol cans. They landed a few feet from where we had just come from, and then he fired at them. The explosion was huge. Not only did they ignite and create a massive fireball but the explosion caused the BBQ gas cylinder to explode. The sheer force caused several of the windows around to break and it sent the group of skinheads with Markus rushing for cover.

We didn't stop to look back. We entered the forest and sprinted as fast as we could around trees, over rocks and through the stream. Even when I felt like I was going to throw up a lung, we kept going. If I slowed, Corey would grab me and pull me on. Likewise, I did the same. All three of us kept running until we had made it through the forest to the lower east side of Mount Pleasant.

The journey back to the address of a home on the east side consisted of a lot of stopping and starting. We hid behind a group of vehicles and spent half an hour inside one of the homes until a group of armed skinheads passed by.

When we made it inside the gate of the address Murphy had given, Murphy came out. His eyes were wide but his reaction didn't come close to the one that Kiera had when she saw her mother. Both of them sobbed hard. Kiera collapsed into her mother's arms. There on the floor she rocked back and forth with her.

"It's okay, I'm here now," Kate kept saying. Ally came out handing us a bottle of water each. I chugged it down and then placed my hands on my legs so I could catch my breath. I was overheated, sweat trickled down my face and my legs were burning from where the wet jeans had chafed my skin.

Kate glanced up at us and mouthed the words, thank you.

EXODUS

The arguments began an hour after we made it back. The group was divided on what to do. One half wanted to leave town, the other, remain and fight.

"You are crazy. If we go now we can get out of here alive. If we stay they are going to kill every single one of us," one of the older women said.

Not all of those who had been in City Hall at the start were inside the room. Some had been killed, others we assumed had sought shelter in one of the homes on the west side. There was too much risk involved trying to find them all.

Kate wanted the skinheads to die for what they had done to her daughter. Murphy was trying to keep her calm.

"Kate. I would want them dead as well but the only reason we've stayed this long was to get you and our kids. We have them. It's time to go."

"Where?"

"I've managed to get hold of Dan, we are going to meet up with him an hour outside of the town."

"Then what? Hide out? How long are we going to survive? This is our home. You just expect me to walk away from here after what they did to Kiera?"

Luke, Billy, Corey and I sat off to one side listening. The idea of being forced out of our town pissed me off but I wasn't prepared to lose my life over it.

"She has a point, Murphy," McCabe added. "We are still officers. It's our job to control this situation."

Murphy shook his head. "I'm all for fighting if there is a good reason. But right now common sense tells me it's best for us to retreat. Wait this thing out. We don't know how many cities have been hit, how bad the fallout is or whether or not the military is coming but if we stay here, we are not only risking our lives but our kids."

"I'm not a kid," Billy said.

"No you're a piss pot," Luke remarked and then chuckled. "Anyway, do we get a say in the matter?"

"No!" the others resounded.

"This affects us as much as you all. I say we go and kill every damn one of them."

Murphy shook his finger at Luke while staring at Kate. "Seriously, Luke, if we make it out of this, I'm going to suggest the court puts you back in the program for at least six months."

"Best of lucking convincing the judge. I saw him laying face down on Bank Street in a puddle of his own blood."

A silence crept over all of us.

"Why the hell are they doing this?" Wayne Layman asked. No one answered. He then turned to me. "You. I'm speaking to you."

I raised my eyebrows and pointed at myself. "Me? How the hell am I supposed to know?"

"You are one of them. You dress like them, you hang out with them. Hell, I saw you set on fire that car down on River Street last month. You have to know why they are doing this?"

"Sorry. I don't."

That obviously was not the answer he was looking for. He edged his way over through the crowded room and stuck his finger into my chest. "How do we know you aren't still with them?"

"That I can answer. You're still alive, dickhead."

He grabbed a hold of me by the collar. "You know your problem?"

"Hey!" Brett said quickly stepping in between.

"You're defending him now?"

"He told you. He's not with them."

"And you believe him? Huh! The same guy who sent him to a program because he was out of control."

"Actually it was court ordered."

Murphy spoke up. "Wayne, lay off."

Wayne owned a convenience store down on Second and River Street. He wasn't lying when he said that I was one of the group that lit a car on fire. It was idiotic but in a small town, late at night, tanked up on liquid courage, shit happens. I didn't light the fire but I was there.

"No, he's right. I was there that night."

McCabe was in the middle of talking to Shaw when he turned around.

"I was there. I saw them light that car on fire. But that was then. This is now."

"And you expect me to believe you've changed because you attended a camp in the wilderness for a month?"

"No. Actually I don't. And quite frankly I couldn't give two shits if you believe me or not. But I just risked my ass multiple times since this has kicked off. I didn't need to." I paused. "I've got a target on my back as much as you have. So if you want hold your prejudice against me, go ahead."

Wayne studied me, shook his head and walked out of the room.

Murphy stepped into the middle of the group. "Look, everyone. No one is going to force you to stay or leave. That's your own choice. We aren't in control of your lives. But Dan Adams has a bunker that is north of here. Now it might not be able to support all of us for longer than a few months but the offer is there. If you stay, there is no denying, you are going to be in a fight for your life. These people are not going to stop. I don't know what's driving them. Insanity, a cause or god knows what. But they will come for us."

"What do you think?" McCabe asked me.

"You're asking me?"

"You spent at least a year and a half with them."

"Like I told Wayne. All I know is they want to take back the country. This isn't the only group. This is just a smidgen of the movement that is out there."

"What can you tell us about Eli?" Brett asked.

I pushed away from the wall. "I don't know Eli. I heard them mention him. What you have to know is everything is told to us on an as-and-when needed basis. It's like the military. I was nothing more than a foot solider."

"You mean, their bitch," Luke said.

"What the hell is your problem, man?"

"You. That's what." He stepped forward. "I saved your

ass back there and you act as though I killed two members of your family."

I scoffed. "You've got it all wrong."

"Do I?"

He shook his head and gave a smug grin. There was silence in the room.

"They're not all bad."

"Could have fooled me. I'm pretty sure I saw them stamp to death some guy down on Bank Street, and put a bullet in the head of a mother up on Cedar. But oh, they aren't all bad," Luke said.

I understood. I really did. They were some mean assholes painting the town red but like any group, not all were committed to the cause. The guy who had lit a fire in the car, hadn't wanted to do it. He was pressured into it. It was like any group. Peers could push a person to the edge. Hell, everyone lived on that edge, one way or another. A person didn't have to be aligned to a group that was considered hateful. We all lived our lives on the edge being pushed towards something that maybe deep down we knew we didn't need, or want or wish to become. But no, he couldn't see that. All he saw was the skinhead, the boots, the tattoos. The rest was just details.

Most of the skinheads I had met in the group prior to being sent away to Camp Zero were just looking for a place to belong. Of course, they wouldn't ever say that. But I could see it in their eyes. It was the same look I had in mine. They all came from rough backgrounds; homes that didn't feel like home.

It had taken me a month out of the group to see how wrong I was. To see that it wasn't what they taught that pulled me in. It was the sense of brotherhood. But the truth was, that could be found elsewhere. Until Camp Zero, I didn't realize that. I gravitated to the first group that lured me in. So who were to blame? The skinheads? The dysfunctional family each one came from? Society? Or all of it?

"It doesn't matter now," Murphy said. "What matters is that we work together. So let's put this to a vote. Whoever wants to stay, stay. Whoever want to go, meet me outside."

Murphy left the room and there was silence. Everyone looked at each other with a blank expression. Some of the people were just strangers that I had seen around town. The kind of people who wouldn't have given me a second look if it wasn't for what happened.

Slowly, one by one they filed out and met Murphy in the kitchen and dining area. It was just common sense. No one wanted to die. None of us were killers. If we left we stood a better chance of surviving. Shaw and McCabe were the only ones who remained. As I was leaving I looked back at Kate. I understood why she wanted to stay, and as for McCabe he was born to the job of being a police officer. It wasn't in his blood to turn back, especially after losing those he'd worked with.

I stood at the doorway for a second. I wanted to say something but I didn't think I had earned the right or could have changed her mind. When I joined the others Murphy went back into the living room.

After ten minutes he came out and both Shaw and

McCabe were with him. I don't know what he said to her to change her mind but she went over to her daughter and hugged her.

"Okay, listen up," Murphy said motioning for everyone to draw in close. "We are going to have to hike out of here. It's going to be a long walk. We will cut through the forest to avoid detection. Those of you who know how to handle a firearm, make yourself known to McCabe. We have three rifles that can be used. If you have any questions, ask them now."

"What about food and water?" a woman asked.

"Yeah."

"We'll take a few cans, and bottled water but be prepared to drink from the river."

"I'm not drinking from the river. What if the fallout has contaminated it?"

"Based on the information Sam provided, we are under the assumption that they targeted the major cities in each of the states. As far as we know the streams and rivers around these parts should be okay."

"Assumptions? As far as you know? You want us to risk our lives based on assumptions?"

"We're not asking you to do anything. We are not in charge of your lives. You don't want to drink, fair enough, but don't blame us when you're thirsty."

With that said he turned and had Luke help him gather up what they could from the cupboards. It was mostly noodles, cans and granola bars. Once several bags were filled, we moved out. We were on Maple Street, two streets over from the direction Murphy wanted to go. Thick trees surrounded all three streets. As McCabe opened the back door and stepped outside, the crack of a gun resounded.

In that instant, McCabe fell. Blood poured from a gaping hole in the front of his skull.

"Get back in," Murphy screamed as more gunfire erupted.

RAPID FIRE

It was too late. Two of the older women collapsed under a hail of bullets. Forced back into the house each of us scrambled to take up a position on the ground or upper floor. Murphy was yelling for us to get down. Drywall and glass flew through the air as the skinheads on the outside kept the house under rapid fire.

Down on the ground I saw Ally with her hands on her head. Not a single one of us dared to stand up. From where I stood I could see those who been killed; two older ladies in their mid-fifties, Wayne and McCabe. Another older guy who ran Tony's Pizza Place in the downtown was in tears. He had his hands over his ears and was yelling.

"I can't take this. I've got to get out."

Murphy was trying to get him to calm down but he was going to snap any minute. Wild-eyed and shaking like mad he rose to his feet and tried to make a break for the front door. He didn't even make it four steps when bullets took him down.

All that remained was myself, Brett, Jodi, Corey, Luke, Billy, Ally, Sara, Kiera, Shaw and Murphy.

When the bullets stopped, all that could be seen inside was drywall dust. It looked like someone had taken a huge bag of flour and scattered it all over the place. Our clothes and faces were covered in it. In those few seconds of quiet we assumed they were reloading their weapons. Murphy signaled for Luke, Corey and myself to take the upstairs.

"Position yourselves either side of the windows. Lay down heat from above. Billy, Brett, you head into the kitchen area. Kiera, Ally, Shaw and myself will keep eyes on the front and back doors. Whatever you do, do not let them breach the yard."

"What about the doors?"

"Don't worry about that. For now get your ass upstairs."

Bolting towards the stairs, Luke, Corey and I double-timed it up. The bedrooms were in a better state. The windows were still intact but not for long. Corey went over to the front of the house, while we focused on the back. Either side of the windows we crouched down and waited, then I peered out. It was hard to see what was going on because the forest smothered anyone who was hiding. It was dense and very dark even in daylight.

"Do you see anything?"

"No movement."

I reached for the handle on the window and popped the latch. I then pushed it open and waited for more gunfire. Luke had a two-way radio in his hand. He pressed it to communicate with the downstairs.

"Murphy, come in."

"Go ahead."

Luke looked out. I saw three at eleven o'clock.

"We need to get out of here," Corey said across from us, just down the hallway.

"Right. Cause that worked for Tony," I said. "At least here we have a chance."

"For how long? Those guys are going to tell the rest of

their asshole friends and they are all going to show up here."

"Corey, we are not the only ones alive in this town. Unless they saw all of us, chances are they will think we are just another group of survivors. They will treat us the same."

"Like?"

"Meaning they will do their job and move on to the next house."

He let out a laugh. "I don't like this."

"Well, I don't exactly fucking love it but we are in this mess," Luke said checking his magazine. He cast a glance over to me.

"Just my luck that I ended up with you. Hey Corey, you want to swap positions?"

"What's that supposed to mean?" I replied.

"It means I don't like you, skinhead."

"Is that what this has come down to?"

"You should be out there with them. At least that way I could put a bullet in your head."

Even Corey looked perplexed.

"Look, I don't know what your deal is with me but I think by now you should know I'm not the enemy."

I peered over to the window and saw one of the skinheads advancing on the back gate. I brought the AR-15 up and was about to take the shot when the guy went down. I looked over to see Luke had taken the shot.

"I had him."

"Yeah, right."

"Guys, stop arguing," I heard Murphy yell up.

"Just like last week, eh, Murph?" Luke hollered back.

Days ago we were in the heart of the wilderness in northern Idaho. Our time was spent hiking, scaling cliff walls and setting up camp. Besides the evenings, we were always in a constant state of motion. Murphy believed that it not only kept us occupied but it was a great way to purge the mind of all the junk, negativity and crap that we lugged around with us. Depending on the day, hell, even the hour, any one of us twelve could have been at each other's throats for some reason. One guy would sit on his ass and say he wasn't going to walk another inch, another guy would throw away his food and say he was going to starve himself if they didn't let him go home, and others would just look for a reason to start a fight.

That was Luke.

I had twisted my ankle coming down into a ravine and Dan asked Luke to carry my backpack. He refused and kicked up a stink. If it was anyone else, he wouldn't have minded but he wasn't going to carry no neo-Nazi skinhead's bag.

Dan like Murphy would try to help each of us to see the commonalities and overlook our differences. He said it was our commonalities that made us strong. My mind drifted back to a week ago.

"Anyone can find fault in a person, but I would challenge you to see what is good about that person."

"Good?" Luke replied. *"There is nothing good about this guy. He's a fucking asshole."*

"And what, your not?" Corey had on numerous times

come to my defense. I think in some ways Corey felt as though he was like me. Luke was another version of Billy according to Corey. That was someone who couldn't see their own faults but would spend all day picking on others.

"You don't want to carry his backpack?" Dan asked.

"No. Why should I?"

"Fine, you don't have to carry his backpack."

Luke got this look on his face as though he had won some competition.

"You'll carry him."

"What?" he yelled back.

"Put your bag down and pick Sam up. You will carry him until you can come up with three things that are good about him."

I tried hard to hide my amusement. I was massaging a sore ankle at the time. The others looked equally amused by it.

"Screw that. You can't make me do that."

"Then we just sit here until you are ready. Our new supplies are at the next rendezvous point."

301

Dan tossed his bag down and sat on top of it.

"Suits me fine," Luke said. "I needed a rest."

An entire day passed before Luke started to realize that Dan meant it. We were not going to move until he picked me up and found three good things to say. After twenty-four hours, we were all starting to get hungry. When we reached day two the others offered to carry me.

"No. Luke is going to do it."

This then led to the others trying to convince him.

"Come on Luke, just do it. Make something up."

Now most would have done that. They would have swallowed their pride and said three random things even if they didn't believe them. Not Luke. I began to realize that this wasn't about getting him to say something good. It was about breaking an internal wall that Luke had erected inside of himself. The very act of picking me up would have meant he had to get close and feel the weight of his own words.

By the time evening rolled around, Luke could tell that if he didn't do it, the others were going to turn on him. They had already begun to cuss him out and one of them had *tossed a water canister at him. They told him he was selfish. As another four hours passed, Luke began looking my way. I could imagine the wheels of his mind churning over. He knew it meant swallowing his pride.*

"God, I'm hungry," Billy said. "Come on, Luke, I swear if you don't pick him up I am going to…"

"Going to what?" Luke rose to his feet and loomed over Billy trying to intimidate him. "If I do it, I do it for myself. Not because you, Dan or any one of these assholes tell me. I do it because I want new supplies. You hear me?"

Dan smiled and nodded his head. With that Luke came over and bent at the hip.

"Well come on, Frost, get on. I don't have all day."

I was tempted to kick him up the ass but instead I hopped on. The funny part was my ankle had started to feel better half a day before that. I didn't tell Dan, as I wanted to see what Luke was going to say about me. I think all of us were keen to know what words he would summon.

Everyone picked up gear and we hauled ass out of there.

To add insult to injury I decided to hum the tune "He

Ain't Heavy, He's My Brother" in his ear for the first five minutes. Billy overheard and started singing the lyrics which only pissed off Luke that much more.

"Come on now. You can put him down as soon as you can come up with three positive things to say about him."

"This is fucking stupid," Luke replied.

"Hold up a second," Dan said walking over and picking up a rock and placing it in Luke's pocket. Any time he cussed he had to carry another one. He carried me for ten minutes before he started huffing and puffing.

"Okay. Sam, you…"

He searched for the words. But the guy couldn't find anything good to say about me. It was hilarious. The others didn't mind because at least we were moving. Maybe not at the speed they wanted but it was better than the way we had spent the past day and a half.

"What was that?" Dan cupped a hand to his ear.

"Look, I can't think of any," he dumped me on the ground, "and I'm not carrying him anymore. You can do whatever you like but I'm done." He slumped down in a

heap. "I will carry his backpack but not him."

Dan crouched down beside him. "Pick him up."

"No. You can't make me."

"Pick him up."

I stepped in and placed a hand on his shoulder. "Dan, it's okay, just leave it."

"No. Pick him up," he said to Luke in a louder tone. I glanced over to Murphy who was chewing on a piece of beef jerky. He didn't seem at all bothered by this. Was this some kind of mind game they were playing? We could never tell what they were up to. Since we had arrived at the camp, they had constantly been placing us in situations that made us question their mental state.

"Fuck you, Dan," Luke replied.

"Okay, fair enough, have it your own way. Everyone else here will take turns carrying Sam."

"What?"

Protests were blurted out among the others. Everyone gave Luke the look of death.

"Come on, Luke, you do it."

Luke didn't say anything; he picked up his bag and strolled on. One by one the others took turns even though I had told Dan I was ready to walk. He wouldn't let me walk. Ten minutes passed, then an hour and Luke dumped his bag down.

"Okay. Okay. I will carry him."

This time when he picked me up, within a matter of minutes he said three things about me that he admired. He admired the fact that I hadn't run away even though I had been bounced from foster home to foster home. According to him, it meant I was resilient. He admired the fact that I had tried to help him when Dan was going off on him even though he had been a jerk to me. He said it meant I had empathy. Finally he said he admired the fact that I hadn't said one bad thing about him being an emo. Did he mean any of it? Fuck no. Did the experience change him? No. But it got him thinking about the group, about his actions and in some ways I think that was all Dan was trying to do. Make him think about his actions and anyone else but himself.

"Earth to Frost. Come in, Frost. Why do you keep spacing out?"

Luke glared at me. He clicked his fingers in front of my face.

I peered out. I could still see at least four more skinheads in the trees with AK47s. One of them tried to light a Molotov cocktail and toss it but someone on the ground floor shot him and the thing dropped and set the guy on fire. He was rolling around on the floor while his buddies tried to put him out.

Corey shuffled down the corridor and joined us in the room.

"Dude, what are you doing? Go back to your position."

"You got a cigarette?"

"You don't even smoke," I said.

"This is nerve-wracking. Have you?"

Luke snorted, reached into his pocket and fished one out for him. He lit it and Corey began having a coughing fit. Both of us started laughing. The second that Luke saw me laughing he scowled again. It was as if he didn't want me to think that he was anything more than some downer guy who covered his face in black shit, grew his hair long and hated skinheads. He certainly didn't want to be seen laughing with one.

"I'm going to check on Murphy," Luke said shuffling away. He glanced back at me momentarily and then disappeared down the stairs.

"What's his deal?" I asked Corey.

"His old man got the shit beaten out of him down at the local bar by a bunch of skinheads."

"But I thought he didn't like his old man?"

"He doesn't but you know how things are. A person says one thing, they think another. That's why he doesn't like you."

"That's quite a broad brushstroke."

"We all do it. Look how many people hate on folks like me."

"So you have a little more weight on you. That's nothing compared to being seen as a white supremacist."

"I guess so." Corey looked out the window and fired a couple of rounds at the tree line.

I hurried over and looked out. "Did you see any?"

"No, but it just lets those fuckers know who's boss."

I laughed.

"Anyway. So are you one?"

"One what?"

"A white supremacist?"

"No. That's like saying every Muslim is a terrorist."

"That's a bit extreme," Corey replied taking another look outside.

"I'm just saying that just because I ran with them it doesn't mean I believed every word that came out of their mouth. Like that guy, back at the old people's residence, the one that you caught with Kiera."

"Oh yeah, that fucker."

I stared at him.

"Why did you hesitate back there?" Corey asked.

"He was a friend of mine."

"Nice friend to have. Do you usually hang out with

rapists?"

"No. I didn't think he would do that."

Corey took another puff of his cigarette and coughed again.

"You should probably give up before you get started."

"I agree." He tossed it out the window and then coughed again. He looked at me. "So what was he like?"

"Maybe he was just recruiting me but I never got that vibe with him. He always said that he didn't agree with everything they taught. Hell, he was the one that told me it was all hot air. The days of skinheads were long over, according to him."

"He believed that?"

"Who knows? Like I said, he wasn't like the others. I don't know what got into him. Maybe he was told to go do it."

Corey screwed up his face. "Who the hell would tell another person to go rape someone? And who would even do it? Bullshit. He did it because she was tied up and there was no one around to stop him. Filthy bastard, if you hadn't been there I would have killed him."

"Hey. I don't condone. You asked why I hesitated."

We returned to looking out the window. Luke came back up the stairs. "Sam. Murphy wants to talk to you."

I nodded, staying low to the ground as I shuffled towards the door. When I made it downstairs, Shaw was near the front door keeping an eye out while Murphy was near the back with Ally and Sara. Kiera was with Billy and Brett. Every few seconds there would be another series of shots and we would find ourselves prone on the ground or seeking cover behind anything that wasn't paper-thin.

"You wanted to speak to me?"

"Yeah, look, we are going try and get back to City Hall. My truck is there. I've radioed to Dan to update him on our situation. We have got to get out of here. If we can't get out, Dan will come in with the others."

"The others?"

"He returned the other guys from camp to their hometown but most of the families were already gone. He dropped off some, but the other five are with him. They have weapons that he had in his truck. If needed they can be here within the hour."

"I think we are going to need it as it looks like they called for backup."

I motioned with my head towards the door. At the foot of the gate was a large group of skinheads. Three times the size of the one that was originally there.

SKINHEAD

"Holy shit," Billy said. "Murphy. Murphy." He turned around and Billy had ducked down behind the window near the front of the house. He was motioning with his thumb. Staying low to the ground both of us moved over there. Brett took up position where Murphy was alongside Shaw. Out front, in the street, standing on top of cars and filling any space available were skinheads. Even more were around back. Some of them were carrying guns. Others, Molotov cocktails, baseball bats and chains.

"How much ammo you got?" Murphy said to Billy, not taking his eyes off the crowd that was slowly building in number.

"Five magazines."

"They are going to set this place on fire, aren't they?" Billy said.

"You think?" I replied. I didn't know for sure but

that's what I might have done. Smoke us out. Even if we didn't come out we would die from smoke inhalation.

"Fuck!" Murphy slammed his fist into the drywall. "Barricade the doors with the furniture."

I shouted up to Luke and Corey to come and help us. They rushed down and we moved what furniture we could to the front and back doors. The back doors were harder to get at as the bodies of Wayne and the two women were blocking up the entryway. We dragged them back and closed the door. I knew it wasn't going to hold. Meanwhile Murphy was on the radio calling for Dan.

"Dan, that help. We are going to need it."

I could hear him filling Dan in on the situation. Kiera took the gun from Wayne's hand. No one said a word. Everyone was going to help if we were to live through this. Brett and Luke shoved a cabinet in front of the main window. It probably wouldn't hold them off if they rushed the house but it would prevent Molotov cocktails from getting in. Well, that was the hope. My bets were on us dying a horrible death. I rushed upstairs and got in position at a window. Murphy thought our best bet was to take the vantage point above them.

"Maybe we can use these?" Corey had found a box of Snapple bottles under the stairs. Some of the bottles had already been drunk. He then returned from the alcohol cabinet with various bottles of alcohol.

"It will do. Billy, give him a hand."

From outside we heard someone's voice over a speaker. I popped open the window to hear what they were saying.

"We'll make this real easy for you."

They wanted to avoid further bloodshed. They wanted Jodi and Brett, along with Luke. Of course they used racial slurs to get their point across.

"Do that, and we'll give you free passage out of here."

Billy cracked up laughing. "This guy must think we are idiots but, I'm all for giving up Luke."

"Fuck off," Luke said.

"They are just toying with us."

Murphy shouted out. "No deal."

"Come on now. I am not going to extend this offer for

long. You decide. We kill three of you or we kill all of you."

"I don't get it. I thought white supremacists wouldn't attack white people?"

"The Jews were white, numb nuts," Luke replied.

"Race is the furthest thing from their minds. We've killed too many of them."

Murphy never replied. From the window I could see Bryan Catz talking to the man they called Eli. He muttered something into his ear and the guy nodded. He brought the megaphone back up to his mouth.

"It's come to my attention, you have a skinhead in the house. Sam Frost, do you hear me?"

None of us said anything.

"Come on now. We know you are in there."

"What do you want?" I yelled out the window. He grinned and looked up towards the front of the house.

"Are you really going to spit in the face of those who helped you?"

"Helped? You guys tried to kill us."

"A little death here, a little death there. I'm surprised you are in there and not out here. Now, I know you have had some issues. I know you didn't choose to be placed with your foster parents." He made some racial remark. "So I am going to offer you a deal. I will pardon what you have done under the umbrella of a misunderstanding. You send on out those I've asked for and no harm will come to you."

By this point Brett was in the same room as me. I stared at him and he dropped his chin.

"And if I do that? You will let the others go?"

Brett frowned. "Sam."

I didn't look at him.

"You have my word," Eli shouted back. I looked back at Brett.

"I need time to think about it," I yelled.

"Time isn't something you have a lot of," he replied.

"What about if I just come out? Will you let all the others go?"

I heard him laugh. "Oh now you can't be serious.

317

Now you are pushing your luck. No deal. So what is your answer?"

"Pretty simple really," I looked at Brett and brought up my AR-15 just below the window. "Fuck you."

With that I opened fire sending the whole group rushing for cover and returning fire. At the same time, from the other room Billy, Murphy and the others began opening fire. Glass shattered around us as they unleashed a torrent of gunfire. Corey and Luke rushed downstairs when they heard someone trying to break in through one of the windows. I dashed down behind them in time to see them standing over the body of a skinhead.

"Here, help me carry these up." Corey gave me three of six bottles that he had turned into homemade Molotov cocktails. I raced upstairs and dispersed them out to the group. Within a minute they were lit and tossed out of the windows, creating a wall of fire. It wouldn't hold them off but it might make it harder to get close. Not every window downstairs could be covered by furniture. The front and back doors were closed, and the front window was blocked but the rear kitchen and living room windows had no glass in the frames.

When I rushed down to get more Molotov cocktails, Billy was holding two and tossing them out the window. As he went to throw a third, a bullet hit him in the shoulder and he collapsed to the floor writhing in agony. I wrapped an arm around him and literally dragged him out of the living room and upstairs. Murphy went down to help Corey and Luke while Sara, the two girls, Shaw and Brett went back and forth exchanging fire with anyone who got close to the house.

"Use your rounds sparingly."

When I brought up Billy he was yelling in agony. I remembered Murphy when he was hit and this didn't even come close. Sara immediately began working on him in the bathroom while I took her place by the window. It was working to some degree. By firing at them they couldn't get close enough to get the Molotov cocktails to hit the house. The closest they could get was about five feet from the perimeter and that was only helping us as it just created a circle of fire that others couldn't cross

The whole thing felt like something out of *Black Hawk Down*. We were stuck with no way out and our ammo was going down by the second. There had to have been at least a hundred and twenty. They knew we would eventually run out of ammo so they would rush around in the trees trying to get us to fire at them and waste ammo.

"This can all be over, Sam. Last chance," Eli hollered over the megaphone.

I stared at him. Eli looked exactly like the others but a lot older. He had to have been in his early fifties. He had a tattoo of a dragon that went from his head to his neck and down beneath his green bomber jacket. A bull's-eye covered one of his eyes and a swastika was on his chest.

"How long do you think it will take until Dan and the others get here?" Luke asked Murphy.

"Less than an hour."

"I hope they get here soon."

TIMBER

I'm not sure at what point I stopped counting the dead. Bodies lay sprawled out on the ground, their faces captured the last thought that passed through their mind. Was it worth it? This was a war that no one was winning. The walls, homes and streets were painted with the blood of people of all ages. For what?

They would have said that our government was to blame. And they would have been right, to some degree. If fear wasn't so prevalent in our world, anti-missile systems wouldn't have been required.

The fact was this was a snowball effect of hatred, racism and division among humanity itself. America was no better than Germany or any country in the world but its constant need to place itself above the shoulders of others had caused all manner of people to react. But it wasn't even America, as it was humanity itself killing humanity.

As bullets penetrated the walls and faces of agony twisted before me, I wanted to push the noise out. I wanted it to end.

Like any war, there were moments of intense shooting, rushing around and yelling as each side tried to take ground, and kill another. If it hadn't been for the brick walls of the house, we would have surely all been dead hours ago.

"What are they doing?" Corey said to me. I peered over the edge. The group out front had backed away. Tired of losing men they had retreated behind a line of cars. The fight was not over. They were reassessing the situation. Searching for any way to get in without being set on fire or shot. It was as if our position on the second floor of the home was like a castle on top of a hill. Even though we were outnumbered, we had the advantage. No matter how hard they tried to get close, they couldn't get inside. Billy, Luke and Murphy held the ground floor with Brett and Jodi while Corey, Ally, Sara, Kiera and myself remained on the second floor.

In a real war the enemy would have bombed the house or rushed it and taken the loss. But that wasn't the case here. While they called themselves foot soldiers, none of them were stupid enough to run at a live gun. Until recent events, their attacks on society amounted to rallies, hate-filled propaganda and the occasional act of violence.

We used the few moments of quiet to check ammo, and make sure that each of us were okay.

"How you doing, Billy?" Murphy shouted up.

He groaned. "My father used to go on at me about working for the family business. I hated it. Right now I would trade in this pain for back-to-back shifts if it meant not feeling this."

"Suck it up, Manning, you little bitch," Corey said smirking at him.

Billy flipped him the bird.

I glanced back out. There was no movement. For the first thirty minutes they had thrown everything they had at us. It was touch and go. I had never felt my heart beat so fast. Molotov cocktails, bullets and even a hammer came flying through the window but they never gained ground.

"What do you think they are doing?" Corey asked.

"Waiting us out," Ally replied. She held in her hand a Glock.

I couldn't even begin to think of the psychological damage this had on all of us. In a period of forty-eight hours we had gone from being delinquent teens pushed away from family and community to having no option but to break laws in order to survive.

"Seems almost ironic, doesn't it," I said.

"What does?" Ally asked peering out the corner of the window.

"This. Working with your father in order to survive."

"Shit happens."

"Don't let your old man catch you saying that. He'll make you pick up a rock and carry it a mile or two," Corey added.

She let out a chuckle. It was the first time I had seen her smile since this had kicked off.

"What are you laughing about?" he asked.

"Would you believe me if I told you that was my idea?" Ally replied.

Corey scowled at her. "Your idea?"

"My father wanted input on the program. He was saying how everyone was swearing all the time. I suggested having people pick up a rock each time they swore and carry it. It would serve as a reminder."

"Like putting a dollar in a swear jar."

"Exactly. Let it hit you where it hurt."

"Thanks, I picked up thirty-seven rocks over the period of that month. My backpack weighed a ton."

"But it worked, right?'

"It didn't stop me swearing if that's what you mean."

"No, but it got you thinking before you spoke."

"Are you telling me that was the point of it?"

"Of course," she replied pulling her gun away from the window. "My father couldn't care less if you swear. Everything they did at that camp was to get you to think about your actions. To think about what it was you did to get there and the consequences."

Corey laid his rifle on the window and peered through the scope. "Alright, Ms. Perfect."

She narrowed her eyes at him.

"Don't pay attention to him, he's just pissed off because he thought your old man had it in for him."

"Whatever," Corey replied before turning his attention to the ground below.

"Murphy, are you seeing this?" Shaw called out to him. I got up close to the window and looked out. The skinheads were pulling back.

"Same over here," Sara said.

At the front and back of the home they moved back slowly until within a matter of minutes they were out of sight.

"Think they are trying to lure us out?"

"Possibly."

Another ten minutes passed. There was no movement and no one was out there.

"Perhaps they got a whiff of your BO, Corey," Billy

said before letting out a laugh only to groan in pain. Luke came up the stairs to get a better look.

"I say we venture out. Might be the only chance we get."

While we had taken out a large chunk of them, there still had to be at least eighty remaining out of the original group two hundred and forty. They could have been anywhere.

"No, we stay here until dusk or Dan arrives. Whatever comes first."

Whenever someone came up, one of us went down to take their place. We had no idea what the skinheads planned but it was obvious they weren't the kind of people to back down.

In the distance we could hear gunfire.

"You think that's Dan?" I asked Murphy. There was a look of concern on his face. It was possible. We had been here for close to two hours. That would have given Dan plenty of time to arrive. It might have been the reason they pulled back. I could see he was itching to find out while at the same time weighing the risk factor.

"Scot." Sara tossed him a look and shook her head. "Don't."

"And if he's out there?"

They exchanged glances and it was clear to see the reason why their marriage might have suffered. Murphy didn't seem like the type of person that avoided danger, he was the type of man that ran towards it if it meant saving a buddy. I admired that about him. Long before I was ordered to attend Camp Zero, I had seen Murphy around town. When he wasn't working with troubled teens he plowed snow in the winter with his truck and did odd jobs alongside Dan.

"Shaw, you want to come with me?"

"I'll go with you," Luke offered.

"No, you need to remain here. For all we know they might be trying to divide and conquer."

"This isn't Iraq, Scot," Sara added.

"Just keep an eye on our daughter."

Sara chuckled to herself. "Yeah, that's what I've done."

"What?" He spun around and for a brief second I think he was about to lose his shit.

"Mom," Ally tried to intervene. That seemed to help as Sara walked into the next room.

"I'm going with you," I said.

"Didn't you hear me? Stay here."

I watched them go downstairs and I heard Brett say he would go. From the window they slowly made their way out the back and then disappeared into the tree line. We were all waiting for the sound of bullets but none came.

Five minutes went by and then I began to get antsy.

"I'm going after them."

"Didn't you hear what he said?" Ally replied.

"If they get caught out there, they are going to be glad we showed up."

"And if you get caught out there?" she asked.

"We'll deal with that as and if it happens." I checked the ammo on the rifle and slung the gun around my back. On my way downstairs Luke followed me.

"Where are you going?" I asked.

"If you can go, so can I."

I wasn't going to argue with him. Brett, Murphy and Shaw had left together heading west. Those that remained were Corey, Ally, Kiera, Sara, Jodi and Billy. We stepped over bodies as we navigated our way into the tree line. The dead stared back. I thought I would feel hate or regret but instead I felt nothing except sadness.

I heard Luke's stomach grumble as we trekked through the forest in the direction of gunfire. All of us had eaten the bare minimum. As we got closer to the edge of the forest, we could now see what was happening.

A group of strangers had taken up position on top of a hunting store. We figured they were using whatever they had scavenged to fend off the group of fifty, maybe eighty skinheads. Some were scaling the side of the wall using the fire escape. To make matters worse, Murphy, Shaw and Brett had obviously been spotted as they had taken cover behind a burnt-out truck further down the street.

Crouched down at the edge of the forest, I was trying to figure out the best course of action. Luke wanted to open fire on them but I was certain that if they caught wind that our group was divided, it was possible they might circle around and overtake the house where the others were.

"Follow me," Luke said.

"Where are you going?"

"You'll see."

I shot the others a quick look, and then reluctantly followed him.

We backed up into the forest and Luke sprinted, jumping over fallen trees and ducking low-hanging branches. At this rate, if we didn't get shot, we were going to end up with a mean rash from poison ivy. The damn stuff was all over the place.

We must have been running for at least ten minutes straight before Luke burst out of the forest into a parking lot. It was the rear of the lumberyard that Billy's father owned. A massive place that stored large amounts of timber. Most was piled up in various places around the yard, some of it had been taken, cut and was ready for purchase by construction companies.

"Hurry up," Luke said waving me on. At the rear entrance, Luke fired a few shots at the door and glass exploded. He reached in, unlocked it and we entered. Glass crunched beneath our boots. I looked around the office space. There were computers; filing cabinets and the place had a rustic, well-used look to it. Luke disappeared into a room and then came out jangling keys.

"What's that?"

"Keys to a Hayes truck."

"Doesn't that have a chip in it?"

He brushed past me and looked at me as though I was some kind of idiot. "No, these beauties aren't made anymore. They closed up shop back in the early '70s long before all that computerized shit. I tell you one thing these suckers are solid. Well built. You can't get a better timber truck."

"How the hell do you know about this? This is Billy's old man's place."

"Yeah, I did a summer job here."

"You were planning on getting a job working for the lumberyard?"

He stared back at me. "You really think highly of yourself, don't you, Frost?"

"No. I just didn't imagine you would want to work in a place like this."

We strolled over to a huge, green, twenty-four-wheel truck that was hooked up to a trailer filled with a massive amount of freshly cut tree trunks at least twenty feet long. The only thing that held them in place were six huge steel bars either side. There was no top to it.

"Oh what, because I wear all black? I bet you thought I was going to join a punk rock band or wind up in some crack house with a needle in my arm."

He hopped up onto the side of the truck and opened the door.

"Get in the other side."

"Luke, what the hell are you planning?"

"You'll see."

"Yeah, I would rather you just tell me."

I went around and got in. He started up the engine and it roared to life.

"Buckle up."

"Are you kidding me?"

"Your funeral."

There was something in the way he said it that didn't sound comforting. The truck hissed as we jerked forward and he circled around heading for a gate that was closed.

"You want me to open the gate?" I asked as we got closer.

He looked over at me and smiled and then hit his foot to the accelerator. The truck smashed through the flimsy mesh wire fence. I looked in the mirror to see it dangling from the hinges. Luke let out a sound as though he was at some football game.

"Always wanted to do that."

"Seriously, Luke, what are we doing here?" I gripped the door handle regretting that I had stepped inside.

"Ever gate crash a party?"

He slammed his foot against the accelerator and the

mammoth truck began picking up speed. I brought down the window, as it was hot and stuffy inside. The wind whistled and whipped at our faces, sending Luke's long hair into a crazy dance. It was about a five-minute drive before we would turn on to Main Street.

"I heard what happened to your father."

I don't know why I came out with it. He cast a glance at me as he kept a tight grip on the large wheel.

"I get it."

"You get what?"

"Why you hate them."

He snorted. "What are you trying to be? My buddy or therapist?"

"Neither."

"Look, just because we are working towards the same goal, that doesn't mean I like you. We aren't buddies, and we sure as hell aren't the same."

"I didn't say that."

"No but you were implying."

I scoffed. "Man, you don't let up, do you?"

He shook his head and focused on the road. I decided it was best to drop the topic. The guy had issues, but then so did I. I wasn't stupid enough to think that the trouble between us would be resolved because we had been forced into a situation of fighting alongside each other.

As we got closer to the corner of Main Street I could hear the noise of gunfire.

"When I tell you to jump. You better jump out my side. That's all I'm saying."

I turned my head towards him but then was thrust back into my seat as we came onto Main Street and he hit the gas. Main Street was the long vein within our town. Unless you were at the furthest tip of the east side, you couldn't see all the way down to the end of the west side because there was a rise halfway up. It wasn't much but enough that it would block the vision of those that were heading east.

"Luke."

He gripped the wheel and the truck began to roar. I cast a glance over my shoulder and out through the window. The huge round logs that were anywhere from twenty to thirty feet long were jam-packed together like matches in a box. I kind of figured what he was about to do and now I really wished I hadn't got in. The truck was still sporting some decades-old cassette player. There was a tape partially sticking out.

Luke tapped it in and hit the power on.

"Let's see what this guy was listening to."

I'm pretty certain that both of us thought that rock music was going to blare out the speakers, country even, instead some organ music came on.

"What the fuck is that?" Luke slapped the eject button and tossed the tape out the window. I might have laughed if I found anything about our situation amusing but I didn't. A shot of fear ran through me as we came over the rise going faster than any timber truck should have been going. The look on their faces as we barreled down upon them was pure panic. The skinheads had grouped together behind three vehicles and by the way they were backing up slowly, I had to wonder if they thought they were safe. Seconds before Luke yanked the wheel he pushed his door open. That was all I needed to see. I didn't have my seat belt on or need to hear him yell to get out. I thrust my body sideways after him just as he turned the wheel. Everything happened in an instant. Metal screeched, sparks flew and the trailer crunched against the asphalt as it turned. When the mammoth tree trunks unloaded, the noise was deafening.

I plowed into Luke, and both of us hit the ground. Still clinging to my rifle I smashed my shoulder so hard in the fall I was certain it broke. Tumbling head over heels I came to rest not far from Luke. Both of us looked up instinctively and watched the truck careen sideways, slicing up everything in its path. An explosion like a clap of thunder and the collision of fifty vehicles shook the ground itself. That truck took out lampposts, phone lines, storefront windows and obliterated any vehicle that was in its path.

A plume of smoke filled the narrow street carrying with it dust and tiny particles of tree bark. All gunfire had ceased. For a few seconds after the truck came to a halt, I thought it was over. Then, in an instant gasoline erupted in a fireball engulfing the truck and what remained at the back of the trailer. An explosion and a huge chunk of metal shot into the air, then returned to the ground with a clatter.

STANDOFF

The sound of screaming filled the air. Two skinheads came rushing forward, their bodies engulfed in fire. They dropped and rolled in an attempt to put out the flames but it was useless. Their bodies were covered in gasoline. Within seconds they stopped moving, and there was silence.

Luke and I were still laid out on the ground. I spat out some grit and slowly clambered to my feet, bringing my rifle up in preparation for an attack. But it never came. There were a few shots fired from above but that was it. A quick, sudden burst of gunfire and then nothing. From behind us, off to the right, Murphy, Brett and Shaw came around the burnt-out wreckage that we had seen them taking cover behind.

"Didn't I tell you guys to stay put?"

"You told us a lot of things," I said.

"No, I specifically told you not to follow."

"Where are the others?" Brett asked.

"Back at the house."

He nodded and gripped my shoulder. "I'm going back to make sure they are okay."

He patted Murphy on the back before he rushed off down an alley that would lead to the residential area.

"Whose idea was this?"

I pointed to Luke. "Who else."

Murphy shook his head. "Should have figured."

Luke shook his head. Murphy whistled to the folks who were on the roof. They made some gesture as if to say they couldn't see if there were any alive. Slowly we made our way past the overturned truck and were finally able to get a better look at the devastation. Not only had it taken out multiple stores, lampposts and cars but the logs had crushed many of the skinheads. Occasionally we'd see an arm or leg sticking out. It was a bloody mess.

I heard a groan and in among the smoke and debris there was a guy still alive. His calves and feet were pinned beneath a log. As I approached him he reached up muttering something. Before I could get close to make out what he said, a gun went off. I shot a glance to my side to see Luke. He'd shot him in the head.

"Fuck, dude, do you not have an off switch?"

"You think they would have extended you any mercy?"

"He was pinned, he couldn't have done anything," I said.

"I put him out of his misery."

Murphy came rushing over as he had gone with Shaw towards the building where the other survivors were.

"What's going on?"

I pointed at Luke, then the dead guy. "That's what."

He shook his head. "Luke, head back to the house, make sure everything is okay."

"But I was—"

"Just do it."

Luke muttered to himself as he broke into a jog and headed back to the house. Over the next ten minutes I took in the sight of carnage. As crazy as it might have seemed, it had worked. Of course not all of them had died. Some must have escaped, but the largest number of the skinheads were crushed, burnt up by gasoline or shot by the survivors on the roof as they tried to escape.

Tom Barrington's father was among the survivors. His son climbed down the side of the fire escape. There were six other men with him, all were armed and gazing at the aftermath that filled the street from one side to the next. Among the dead was Eli Pope.

As I stood over his lifeless corpse, he didn't look as threatening as he once had. To think that at one time he had been a kid unaffected by hate. I shook my head. What had changed to send him down this path?

"That was the craziest shit I have ever seen," Tom said walking over. "Now I understand why the court sent you two to a wilderness camp for troubled youth."

Tom stared on with wide eyes and a Winchester rifle slung over his shoulder. As we soaked in the sight, others from the town began to appear. They were gathered together in groups. All of them were carrying a handgun or rifle.

Among them were Dan and five of the guys from the camp. I came to learn that Dan had arrived and upon seeing how many there were, realized that it would have been suicide to attempt to take them on alone. While they were distracted in their attempts to breach the house we were in, he had gone to homes of key people in the community to get them to help. That's what all the gunfire was. From the forest we had only seen a few of them on the roof firing down on skinheads, but out of view were others in windows, doorways and alleys.

The community had joined together to fight back.

I had to admit it was something else to see. I don't know how many survived the initial onslaught. That would be determined after. But what I did know was there were at least fifty courageous people from the town who were willing to risk their lives.

As folks continued to remain alert, going through the wreckage and checking for anyone who was alive, Luke came bursting out onto the street. He was out of breath and didn't have his gun with him.

"They've taken the house."

"What?" Murphy yelled and immediately broke into a sprint. I chased after him, looking back to see another twenty from the fifty coming to help. Along the way Luke was trying to explain but he could barely get a clear word out.

"A group of them must have seen us leave and doubled back to the house."

"How many are there?"

"Maybe six, eight at the most? If I hadn't seen one through the window, I would have walked right in there."

"What about Brett?"

"I think he's inside."

My thighs protested as I ran towards the house thinking the worst. When we arrived, we didn't even get twenty feet from the door when they opened fire on us. In a hail of bullets, we dived for cover behind the same vehicles that they had used. Murphy directed the twenty to go around to the back while we approached the front. As we came into view, they were already waiting for us.

"How's it feel to have the tables turned, Frost?" Bryan Catz shouted down.

"Let them go," Murphy shouted. Behind Bryan, Markus stood with Sara and Ally. His men had their weapons on them and on the occupants of the house.

Markus pushed Brett near the front of the window almost sending him out. "You don't tell us what to do, soldier boy." He gestured to his men to bring the others to the window. They shoved forward Sara, Ally, Kiera and Billy. Beside them were Brett and Jodi. It was almost like they wanted to use them like a shield in the event that we had ideas to fire at them. Markus moved from side to side behind them with a handgun pointed at the back of their heads, taunting us.

"Don't do this," Murphy shouted up while slowly moving forward. "Let's talk."

Markus scoffed at the idea. "Talking ended a long time ago, old man. I would have thought the bombings made that clear."

"Just tell us what you want."

He let out a laugh. "Guy wants to know what we want. I'll show you what we want." Markus pushed Jodi forward, raised his gun and shot her in the back of the head before anyone could even react. My eyes widened. A fight ensued inside as Brett turned on his captors, and the others did the same. Several gunshots were fired.

"Go. Go!" Murphy shouted.

What occurred next was pure anarchy. From the front and back of the house we pressed in. We all knew that if we didn't get in there fast this wasn't going to end well for anyone. A skinhead came into view at a lower window, and I fired at him while launching in the air. One by one we piled into the house. I saw three of the survivors who had chosen to come with us get shot. One had been blasted in the face.

Like a team of military clearing a home, our crew moved together as one unit. By the time we made it to the second floor, Bryan Catz was gone, and so were three others. They had jumped from the window. Markus Wainwright was on the floor strangling Brett when we came in. Murphy slammed the butt of his gun into the back of his head. Four other skinheads holding Sara, Kiera, Ally and Billy released them and backed up, realizing that it was over.

They stood there with their hands up. When Brett got up off the floor, in one smooth motion he took the gun from my hand, turned and fired a round into the head of Markus Wainright. The boom of the gun going off echoed and startled everyone in the room.

Murphy collapsed to his knees beside Sara. She had been shot in the stomach in a struggle for control. She was clinging to her gut as Ally loomed over her crying uncontrollably. What had begun as threats had turned into chaos and blood.

"Shaw," Murphy shouted out. She was on the ground floor. When she came up Murphy had his hands over Sara's stomach. Blood seeped through his fingers. She didn't last long. Within a minute or two her eyes closed and the room was filled with the wails of Ally.

I looked down at Jodi's lifeless body. Brett clung to her

hand, rocking back and forth.

Anger and rage overcame me as my eyes drifted around the room for Bryan Catz. I rushed out of the room and took the steps two at a time, jumping the last four.

"Where are you going?" Luke asked.

I didn't even reply and I certainly wasn't aware that Corey and Luke had followed me until I came into the street. I looked up and down for Bryan but he was nowhere to be seen. Corey and Luke caught up with me.

"He's gone, Sam."

I began jogging down the road.

"Where are you going? He's probably long gone by now."

Though I searched that town for the remainder of the day with Luke and Corey beside me, I never did find Bryan. Though it wasn't him who had fired the shot that killed Jodi, he was in my mind equally responsible.

EPILOGUE

Not all of the two hundred and forty skinheads died in the forty-eight hours after our town was thrown in darkness. It was only in the days after that we discovered that some had deserted the group when the chaos had erupted. When asked why they walked away, they all gave the same answer. They didn't sign up to kill others. Much like myself, they had been drawn into the group through friends, family and acquaintances. They had stayed because they wanted to belong.

Once the threat was gone we could clearly see what remained.

Mount Pleasant was in ruins. It had become a graffiti-soaked, fire-charred and bullet-ridden wasteland. It would take months to rebuild what they had destroyed in those few short days. Even then, the future didn't look bright. The real nightmare had only begun. There was no power and as far as we knew other cities and towns were in the same state. Overrun by skinheads, and swallowed up by darkness and panic.

Back at the gym, Dan had come across a map of the United States detailing where the bombs had been detonated. Along with this was a detailed plan of how the white supremacist group that operated through every state in the country would target military installations, the power grid and satellite defenses in some of the largest cities. Most of the major cities, such as New York, Los Angeles, Jacksonville, Chicago, Seattle, Vegas, Kansas, Atlanta, New Orleans, Laredo and so forth had been targeted. Eighty-four nukes housed in suitcases left over from the Cold War had been used to bring the country to its knees.

"It's hard to imagine that they managed to smuggle that kind of power into the country."

"There were a lot of Russian spies back in the Cold War," Dan said browsing through paperwork that he'd found inside one of the cabinets in the office.

"I always imagined that nuclear bombs going off

meant the end of mankind."

Dan chuckled as he looked through paperwork. "That's one of the many false beliefs that Americans have. If that were the case, preppers like me wouldn't try to make preparations to survive the unsurvivable. Remember these were one kiloton. We aren't talking about the A-bomb blast in Hiroshima."

"But it's still dangerous, right?"

"Of course. Millions will be dead from what they detonated, the radiation in those areas will kill even more, but there will be survivors like us in small isolated towns. And there will be preppers who have entered fallout shelters and are using air pumps to ventilate, and using all manner of devices like fallout meters and removing radioactive iodine from water using settling and filtering."

"You really know your shit," Luke said.

Dan chuckled. "Give it a while and so will you."

"So how long?" I asked.

"The first few weeks after fallout are the most dangerous for those near the blast sites. Thankfully we aren't anywhere near them and any particles from the fallout decay rapidly."

"Yeah, but wouldn't the wind carry some of the fallout further afield?"

"You are right but it depends on the location of the blast, and the nuclear device used. Remember these were one kiloton not like the Tsar Bomba, which was 50 megatons. The initial radiation radius on these may be up to two and half kilometers roughly."

"But radiation can still spread further than that, right?"

I continued looking through files for any information that might give us even more insight into those involved and the enormity of what we were facing.

"Of course, there's nothing to stop it spreading around the word once it hits the jet stream. Close to 1,000 atomic bombs were tested at the Nevada site between the fifties and nineties. And without a doubt it will affect the weather and all manner of things but again it all comes back down to where and what kind of nuclear power we are talking about. One kiloton is peanuts compared to

Hiroshima, but it's still enough to obliterate a lot and leave the country in darkness for a long time."

"Do you think they detonated all eighty-four of them?"

"Maybe, but we have to approach this as if they have."

"So are we still going to your shelter?"

"The offer is on the table. At least it will provide some protection for the next month or two until we can determine the true level of danger that is facing us here. We are going to gather up supplies first and then head out."

"What about the others in the town?"

"We can't take everyone, Sam. And while I think they won't be affected by the fallout from the one that was detonated in Boise, Idaho, I can't be certain. Neither can I fit them all in the shelter. Some people are just going to have to take a chance."

"But you'll help them, right?" Luke asked.

"Of course. We'll make sure they know what not to do and from there they are on their own, I'm afraid. In many ways we all are."

"I wonder if they detonated some these in other countries?" Corey asked.

We used our flashlights to look around. Even though it was day, very little light was flooding the office.

"Who knows?"

In light of the bad news that Dan gave the town, no one initially chose to leave. The few that did, had underground shelters. They had already made plans to take their family and a few close friends. But again, not everyone could or would leave.

A small funeral was held for Jodi and Sara in the Mount Pleasant Cemetery. Brett and Murphy bonded over the death of their partners and in many ways the community itself became close as it worked together to clean up the streets, bury the dead and prepare for the next couple of months in isolation.

Ally said very little in the days after. She stayed close to her father as though he was the last sure thing remaining in her life. Kiera would remain in a state of devastation for months to come. Everyone dealt with trauma in different ways. I was just glad she had her mother beside her.

As for Luke, well, I can't say that Luke and I resolved our differences. I knew time itself might change that, though I wasn't holding my breath. His family was found among the dead and though he tried to hold in his emotion, I saw his eyes well up before he wiped them with the back of his sleeve.

After collecting a sleeping bag from his home, and changing into a different set of clothes, he gave us the sign that he was ready to leave.

Billy squeezed out as much sympathy as he could from everyone after his close brush with death. I had a strong feeling we would be hearing about that bullet wound a year from now. It would become the stuff of legend, and knowing Billy if we encountered any females along the way, he would most likely work in his survivor story as a pickup line.

Corey's mother and sister survived and chose to come

with us to Dan's shelter in northern Idaho. She clung to her son as we loaded up the back of the two trucks with supplies and more ammo.

Seventeen of us left that day.

As we drove away, leaving the small town of Mount Pleasant in the rearview mirror, we had no idea when help would come or if it would. We were unsure about the stability of the country and what the long-term consequences of the damage were.

We were living on shaky ground among a nation that was in a state of panic. And though Dan and Murphy believed we could ride this out and survive, perhaps even thrive, we were all unsure of what to believe.

But two things we clung to for now.

We were in this together.

This wasn't the end, only the beginning.

A Plea

Thank you for reading State of Panic. If you enjoyed the book, I would really appreciate it if you would consider leaving a review. Without reviews, an author's books are virtually invisible on the retail sites. It also lets me know what you liked. You can leave a review by visiting the book's page. I would greatly appreciate it. It only takes a couple of seconds.

Thank you — **Jack Hunt**

Newsletter

Thank you for buying State of Panic, published by Direct Response Publishing.

Click here to receive special offers, bonus content, and news about new Jack Hunt's books. Sign up for the newsletter. http://www.jackhuntbooks.com/signup/

About the Author

Jack Hunt is the author of horror, sci-fi and post-apocalyptic novels. He currently has five books out in the Renegades series, a time travel book called Killing Time and another called Mavericks: Hunters Moon. Jack lives on the East coast of North America.